FING

Previously written by
David Walliams

THE BOY IN THE DRESS
MR STINK
BILLIONAIRE BOY
GANGSTA GRANNY
RATBURGER
DEMON DENTIST
AWFUL AUNTIE
GRANDPA'S GREAT ESCAPE
THE MIDNIGHT GANG
· BAD DAD
THE ICE MONSTER
THE BEAST OF BUCKINGHAM PALACE
CODE NAME BANANAS

FING
SLIME

THE WORLD'S WORST CHILDREN
THE WORLD'S WORST CHILDREN 2
THE WORLD'S WORST CHILDREN 3
THE WORLD'S WORST TEACHERS
THE WORLD'S WORST PARENTS

Also available in picture book:

THE SLIGHTLY ANNOYING ELEPHANT
THE FIRST HIPPO ON THE MOON
THE BEAR WHO WENT BOO!
THE QUEEN'S ORANG-UTAN
THERE'S A SNAKE IN MY SCHOOL!
BOOGIE BEAR
GERONIMO
THE CREATURE CHOIR
LITTLE MONSTERS

David Walliams

FING

Illustrated by Tony Ross

HarperCollins *Children's Books*

First published in Great Britain by
HarperCollins *Children's Books* in 2019
Published in this edition in 2021
HarperCollins *Children's Books* is a division of HarperCollins*Publishers* Ltd,
1 London Bridge Street
London SE1 9GF

www.harpercollins.co.uk

HarperCollins*Publishers*
1st Floor, Watermarque Building, Ringsend Road
Dublin 4, Ireland

1

ISBN 978–0–00–834911–0

Printed and bound in England by CPI Group (UK) Ltd, Croydon CR0 4YY

MIX
Paper from
responsible sources
FSC™ C007454

For Percy, Wilfred and Gilbert

THANK-YOUS

I WOULD LIKE TO THANK THE FOLLOWING MONSTERS:

ANN-JANINE MURTAGH

My Executive Publisher

TONY ROSS

My Illustrator

PAUL STEVENS

My Literary Agent

CHARLIE REDMAYNE

CEO

ALICE BLACKER

My Editor

HARRIET WILSON

Publishing Director

KATE BURNS

Art Editor

RACHEL DENWOOD

Publisher

SAMANTHA STEWART

Managing Editor

VAL BRATHWAITE

Creative Director

DAVID McDOUGALL

Art Director

SALLY GRIFFIN

Designer

KATE CLARKE

Designer

ELORINE GRANT

Deputy Art Director

MATTHEW KELLY

Designer

TANYA HOUGHAM

My Audio Editor

GERALDINE STROUD

My PR Director

Mr Meek

Mrs Meek

Myrtle Meek

And a **FING**…

?

This is the story of a child who had

everything,

but still wanted **more.**

Just one more

"FING".

PROLOGUE

Sometimes perfectly nice parents have children who are monsters.

Meet the Meeks.

This is Father, Mr Maurice Meek. As his name suggests, Mr Meek is a mild-mannered man. He likes to wear socks with his sandals, and would not dare to eat a peach in public. Mr Meek works as a librarian. He loves **LIBRARIES** as

MR MAURICE MEEK

they are quiet, like him. This is a man who wouldn't say boo to a goose. Or, indeed, any species of bird.

This is Mother, Mrs Meredith Meek. She wears her glasses on a chain round her neck.

MRS MEREDITH MEEK

The most embarrassing moment of her life was when she once sneezed on a bus, and everybody turned round and looked. It will not surprise you to learn that she is also a librarian. Meredith met Maurice at the **LIBRARY**. They were both so painfully shy that they never spoke a word to each other for the first ten years of working there. Eventually, across the poetry aisle, Maurice and Meredith fell in love. Some years later, they were married, and some years after that they had a baby girl.

MYRTLE MEEK

This is their daughter, Myrtle. You might be thinking that nothing could be sweeter than a little baby girl. WRONG! From the moment she was born, Myrtle was an absolute **HORROR**. Whatever she was given – dummies, cuddly toys, rubber duckies – the baby demanded more.

Myrtle's first-ever word was "more", and she uttered it on the very day she was born. It was more milk Baby Myrtle was demanding, even though she had already guzzled a gallon. "More" was a word the infant would say over and over and over again.

"MORE! MORE! MORE!"

Being Meek by name and meek by nature, Maurice and Meredith didn't dare stand up to their monster of a child. Whatever Baby Myrtle wanted, Baby Myrtle got. Her parents bought their baby daughter toys and toys and MORE toys, even though she would instantly smash them to pieces. BISH! BASH! BOSH!

"MORE! MORE! MORE!"

As a toddler, they gave their daughter crayons and crayons and MORE crayons. Myrtle would use them to scrawl all over the walls.

SCRATCH!

Before snapping them in two.

SNAP!

"MORE! MORE! MORE!"

As she grew bigger and bigger and bigger still, Mr and Mrs Meek would feed Myrtle chocolate biscuit after chocolate biscuit after chocolate biscuit. More and more and more. Even though

Myrtle would take great delight in spitting the crumbs back in their faces.

SPLURT!

"MORE!
MORE!
MORE!"

PART ONE

MORE, MORE, MORE

Chapter 1
HOWLING

The years passed. Mr and Mrs Meek secretly hoped that their daughter was just "going through a phase". But this "phase" was not one she ever grew out of. In fact, Myrtle's behaviour became worse and worse* over the years.

The nasty noughts turned into the outrageous

---

* Or "worserer", which is a real word. Just check *The* **Walliamsictionary.**

ones. Then followed the terrible twos, and the tumultuous threes. After the fearsome fours and the frightful fives came the sickening sixes and the spiteful sevens. Then there were the egregious eights and the noisy nines.

Oh my word, they were noisy. Now nine, Myrtle would wake her parents up every morning by howling...

"WWWAAAHHH!

I wanna teddy bear!"

"WWWWAAAAHHHH!

I wanna pony!"

"WWWWWAAAAAHHHHH!

I wanna suitcase full of money!"

The girl would make such a din that the little Meek family house would actually shake.

R A T T L E !

Books would fly off the shelves.

W H O O S H ! BONK!

Pictures would fall off the walls.

DUNK! SHATTER!

Plaster would shower down from the ceiling.

CRUMBLE! DUNK!

Poor Mr and Mrs Meek would be hurled out of bed.

DOOF! DOOF!

They would scramble to their feet, and immediately run around doing their daughter's bidding. They gave Myrtle everything. But everything was never, ever enough.

Oh no.
The girl wanted
one more
"FING".

Chapter 2
AN ALPHABET OF STUFF

Over the years, Myrtle's bedroom became so piled high with stuff her parents had got her that you could barely get in or out. She demanded more and more and more, and she got more and more and more.

Myrtle had at least one thing for every letter of the alphabet:

Ant farm. Home to a million and one ants.

Boomerang that doesn't come back. Myrtle lost that on her first throw.

Cowbell, which the girl put round her mother's neck so she could locate her easily.

Dog-grooming set. Even though she didn't have a dog.

Elf.

Finger puppets of every king and queen of England from 1066 to the present day.

Gravel collection. It was the biggest in Europe.

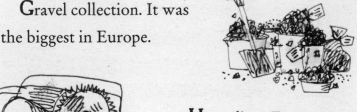

Ham slicer. Even though she hated ham.

Ice skates made for an elephant. Four of them.

XXXXXXXXXXL

Jar containing one of scientist **Albert Einstein's** burps.*

Knee warmers.

Lucky sausage. Actually it was unlucky.

Map of Belgium. A country she had no intention of ever visiting as it was, in her words, "too Belgiumy".

Nelson's Column made out of sultanas. Life-size.

---

*Bought at an auction for thousands of pounds.

Owl fudge. This is fudge
made of melted-down owls.
It is even more disgusting
than it sounds.

Painting of some air.
It wasn't much to look at.

Quicksand. Children
who came over for a playdate and ended up
displeasing Myrtle met their doom in it.

Remote-controlled hedge
(which could reach speeds
of up to one mile an hour).

Stuffed flea. It was so small that it was impossible to see.

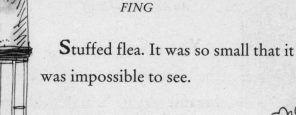

Turnip shampoo. It made your hair smell "as fresh as a turnip".

Underpants for worms. Only come in size "small".

Venom from a poisonous aubergine. Deadly.

Wombat juicer. Perfect for producing a cool, refreshing glass of wombat juice.

Xylophone case. Myrtle didn't want an actual xylophone, just the case for one.

Yeti. It hasn't been sighted in the Himalayan mountains for years because Myrtle kept it locked in her cupboard.

Zebra dung. It was the only thing she could think of that began with a "z".

One thing Myrtle didn't have any of was books. Despite her parents being librarians, she DETESTED books and thought they were B-O-O-O-R-R-R-I-I-I-N-N-N-G-G-G!*

The girl had all this stuff, a universe of junk, but still she wanted something more. The funny thing was that she just didn't know what.

---

* *Myrtle would even have loathed this one, even though it is all about her.*

Chapter 3
FURY

Can you guess what Myrtle demanded for her tenth birthday? In the incredibly unlikely event that you guessed...

A pair of exploding socks.

A life-sized blue-whale bath toy. When it went in the bath, all the water spilled out.

A balloon model of the Taj Mahal.

A pencil un-sharpener.

And a robot pea.

…then congratulations. You were correct and win one pound.*

Mr and Mrs Meek were forced to give their daughter all these things that she had demanded for her birthday. If they hadn't, Myrtle would have howled the house down.

"Happy birthday, our beautiful angel!" they called out as Myrtle lay in bed, ripping open the

---

* *Just write to me to claim your prize of one pound. Please don't forget to include* ONE **BILLION** POUNDS *for postage and packing.*

presents and throwing the scrunched-up balls of wrapping paper back at them.

RUSTLE!

DOINK!

Moments later, she was demanding something more. What was unusual this time, though, was that the girl had absolutely no idea what that something should be. Myrtle had so many things that she couldn't think of a single thing in the world she didn't have.

"I wanna FING!"

she announced over breakfast. The girl was scoffing a ginormous bowl of chocolate ice cream with seventeen chocolate flakes stuck in it, and an ocean of chocolate sauce on top. Yes, Myrtle had chocolate for breakfast. And lunch. And dinner. Well, would you say no to her?

Mr and Mrs Meek, who were dipping their neatly cut soldiers into boiled eggs, shared a worried look. A **"FING"**?

Whatever did she mean?

"A **'FING'**, my dearest darling?" asked Mother, putting down her book, *One Hundred Poems for Ladies*.

"Yeah. Are you deaf? A **FING!**"

"What's a **'FING'**, sweetness?" enquired Father, putting down his book, *One Hundred Poems for Gentlemen*.

"I dunno, but I want one!"

"How do you spell it?" asked Mother.

Myrtle's face went scarlet with fury.

"I ain't fick! You spell it the normal way. F! I! N! G! **FING!**"

The girl thumped the breakfast table with her fist to add emphasis.

BASH!

All the crockery flew into the air, and smashed on to the floor.

CRASH! **BANG!** WALLOP!

"Pick up the pieces! NOW!" the girl ordered.

On their hands and knees under the kitchen table, Mr Meek whispered to his wife, "What are we to do? Our beloved offspring wants a **'FING'**. But I don't think a **'FING'** is a real thing. I worry a **'FING'** is a made-up thing."

"We'll have to think of **SOMEFING** – I mean,

something," replied Mrs Meek just before she felt a boot up her bottom.

BOOF!

"OUCH!" she cried.

"SHUT UP DOWN THERE!" came the voice from above. "I can barely hear myself blow off!"

PPPFFFFT!

"That's better."

Mr and Mrs Meek were in a panic. If they didn't come up with some **"FING"**, there was going to be TROUBLE.

BIG
TROUBLE.

Chapter 4

BESTEST BEST

After breakfast that morning, Mr and Mrs Meek gave their daughter a lift to school. And I mean "lift", literally. Every morning, they were forced to lift her up and carry her there. Myrtle refused to walk even though it

was only a short distance away. It was a mighty effort carrying her. As she mostly ate chocolate, Myrtle was as heavy as an ox.*

"PUT ME DOWN!" Myrtle ordered as her poor parents made their final stagger to the school gates. Once they'd carefully lowered her to the ground, Father passed his daughter her industrial-sized lunchbox. It was so big and heavy it was on wheels.

"Have a lovely day at school, my sweetest of hearts," he said.

"DON'T FORGET – BY THE TIME I GET HOME FROM SCHOOL I WANNA FING!" she bawled, before waddling off into the playground, knocking several smaller children to the ground as she did so.

OOF! OOF! OOF!

"My angel of heaven, we promise we will do our absolute bestest best!" called out Mother brightly.

---

* *A really heavy ox at that. One that might win a rosette for heaviness.*

This stopped Myrtle in her tracks. Slowly she turned round and reached into her lunchbox.

"**BESTEST BEST ISN'T GOOD ENOUGH!**" she hollered. Myrtle pulled out one of the tall cartons of chocolate milk and lobbed it at her mother.

WHIZZ!

SPLAT! "ARGH!"

It hit poor Mrs Meek right in the face, soaking her and her pink flowery dress.

"Thanking you kindly," remarked the lady, not sure what else to say.

Father passed his wife the handkerchief he always kept in his breast pocket.

"There we are, Mother."

Mrs Meek dabbed at the chocolate milk. It was little use. The pink flowery dress was now a brown chocolatey mess.

"BESTEST BETTER THAN BEST!" appealed Father.

Once again, Myrtle reached into her lunchbox.

"Oh dear," muttered Father, closing his eyes as he was sure something was about to be lobbed in his direction.

He was right.

Z O O M !

SPLURGE!

A bucket of chocolate mousse hit him – BANG! – on the top of his head.

"Thanking you muchly!" he said, like his wife, not knowing what else to say.

Without a word, Mother passed the handkerchief back to her husband, and he attempted to de-mousse himself.*

"Don't you worry your pretty little head!" called out Father, lying. There was nothing pretty or little about Myrtle's head. "We will have that **FING** for you as soon as you are home from school."

"YOU BETTER!" replied Myrtle. "Or else."

---

* *Unfortunately, this sort of thing happened every morning to poor Mr and Mrs Meek. Indeed, Father still had a piece of double chocolate cake in his ear from last week's packed-lunch volley, which he had been saving for his lunch.*

Neither Mr Meek nor Mrs Meek knew what "else" was, but, whatever it was, it sounded nasty.

Drrriiiing!

The school bell rang.

As soon as Myrtle began lumbering off towards her classroom, Father took his wife's hand.

"Ooh, you are very forward, Mr Meek," she remarked.

"I know the perfect place to start looking for a **FING**," said the librarian.

"Where?"

"The **LIBRARY**, of course!"

Chapter 5
GIANT POOPS

Mr and Mrs Meek bolted down the street. They were quite a sight, both covered as they were in chocolatey-brown gunge. The pair looked like two giant poops making a dash for freedom.

W H O O S H !

As soon as they reached the doors to the **LIBRARY**, they slowed to a stroll.

PITTER-PATTER...

THE LIBRARY

THE LIBRARY VAULTS

After all, the **LIBRARY** is a place where you should always be on your best behaviour. Especially if you are a librarian.

"W-w-where to begin?" whispered an out-of-breath Father as they strolled through the aisles and aisles of floor-to-ceiling books, leaving a trail of brown sludge behind them. *OOZE!*

"The d-d-dictionary?" replied an out-of-breath Mother.

Their eyes searched the shelves of dictionaries until they found the widest, weightiest one. They eased it off the shelf together. The book was almost as heavy as their daughter.*

Mrs Meek eagerly flicked through the pages until she reached the long, long list of words that began with **F**. However, soon a word that began with **F**, "frustration", was painted all over her face.

"**'FING'** isn't in the dictionary," she whispered.

"OH, FOR GOODNESS' SAKE!" exclaimed Father.

"SHUSH!" shushed Mrs Meek, pointing to a sign that her husband himself had put up, which read "SILENCE".

"Sorry," he mouthed, before continuing in hushed tones. "That doesn't mean there is no such thing as a **'FING'**. There are thousands and

---

* *Almost, but not quite. Nothing was as heavy as Myrtle.*

thousands of books in the **LIBRARY**. Surely one of them must mention a **'FING'.**"

"But what books should we look at next, Father?"

"Well, let's think, Mother. What does a **'FING'** sound like to you?"

Both went into deep concentration.

"A rude-shaped vegetable?" guessed Mother, reaching for THE **BIG BOOK** OF RUDE-SHAPED VEGETABLES

"An annoying board game?" suggested Father as he took down A HISTORY OF ANNOYING BOARD GAMES

"A very distant planet?" said Mother as she found THE UNIVERSE AND BEYOND THE BEYOND OF THE BEYOND

Books, books and more **books** tumbled off the shelves. **Books** about the human body. **Books** about motor cars. **Books** about flowers. **Books** about antiques. **Books** about **books**.

"Could a **'FING'** be that thing that's left in your plughole after a bath?" suggested Father.

"An unidentifiable item of clothing you find in the tumble dryer?" guessed Mother.

Guesses were volleyed back and forth like tennis balls.

"Something sticky you find up your nose that isn't a bogey?"

"A mysterious stain?"

"The gangly bit of a jellyfish?"

"A prize from a Christmas cracker that you never actually work out what it is?"

"Something you find stuck to a dog?"

"That dangly bit of your belly button that looks like the end of a balloon?"

"The fluffy stuff you find between your toes?"

"The opposite of a **'FONG'**?" exclaimed Mrs Meek.

"What's a **'FONG'**?" asked Mr Meek.

"I don't know," she replied, downcast.

Hours passed until the exhausted pair had searched through every single book in the **LIBRARY**.*

Just as they were about to admit defeat and brace themselves for the wrath of their daughter, Mrs Meek had a thought.

"There is one last place we haven't looked," she said.

"Where? Where? Where?" he asked eagerly.

"The ancient vaults of the **LIBRARY**. That's where all the old books are kept. We might find a clue down there."

Mr Meek gulped. "But, Mrs Meek, we librarians are strictly forbidden to go down to the vaults."

---

* *Even my ones. Really, they should have looked through this book, but of course it hadn't been written yet.*

"Everybody is forbidden.
Nobody has been down there
for a hundred years…"

Chapter 6
TWO EVILS

"**W**ell then, we can't go down into the vaults," said Mr Meek. "And that's that."

Mrs Meek was not taking no for an answer. "But what about our darling daughter? If we don't get her a **FING**, there will be tears before bedtime."

"Oh yes." The man turned deathly pale at the thought. His eyes rolled back and he wobbled.

"Are you quite all right, Mr Meek?"

But, before he could reply, Mr Meek fainted. Mrs Meek went to catch him, but they both tumbled backwards and landed on the floor.

THUD!

"OOF!" she exclaimed as her husband landed on top of her.

An old man stepped over them to reach a gardening book. The pair smiled politely up at him.

"Good morning," they said.

"Are you all right under there, Mrs Meek?" enquired Mr Meek.

"Yes. Are you all right?"

"Me?"

"Yes. You fainted."

"Did I?"

"Yes."

"Oh dear."

"Oh dear indeed."

"Let me help you up."

"No, let me help you up!"

This went on for quite a while until finally both of them were on their feet. Now the pair had to choose between two evils. Either they went down to the spooky vaults of the **LIBRARY** or they faced the wrath of their daughter.

The lesser of the two seemed to be the vaults.

"I don't think we have a choice," said Father.

"Then follow me," replied Mother.

Mrs Meek led her husband to a battered old door in the far corner of the **LIBRARY**. Cobwebs covered the cracks, and a sign over it read **"DO NOT ENTER"**.

"Will it be dark down in the vaults?" he asked, his voice wavering.

"Oh yes. Pitch black. To protect all the old books," she replied.

"Well then, ladies first…"

"Me?" protested Mrs Meek.

They were both scared of the dark.

"I insist," he pressed.

"I insist."

"I am a gentleman. I have to let a lady go first."

"No, no, no, that's very old-fashioned these days, Mr Meek. You should definitely go first."

"No, you."

"You."

"YOU!"

The pair had reached something of a stand-off.

"I know! Let's both go together," announced Mother.

"Good plan," replied Father. He took down the rusty old key that was sitting on top of the doorframe. Looking around to check no one was watching, he unlocked the door.

CLICK.

CREAK!

He fumbled for his wife's hand, and together they slowly descended the steps.

"It's not too bad, is it?" asked Mrs Meek.

"N-n-n-n-no,"

stammered Mr Meek.

Chapter 7

ANCIENT, OBSCURE AND BIZARRE

To his relief, Mr Meek found a candle and a box of old matches halfway down the stairs. His hands trembling uncontrollably, he passed them to his wife, who struck a match and lit the candle.

STRIKE!

The flickering light illuminated shelves and shelves of dusty old leather-bound books. The **LIBRARY** vaults were a treasure trove of titles that were ancient, obscure and bizarre. There were thousands of books down there, all of them long out of print.

POISONOUS CHEESES OF THE BRITISH ISLES

Terrifying Tales for Children

THE BUMPER BOOK OF MEDIEVAL TORTURE

HYMNS TO MAKE YOUR EARS BLEED

PAINTINGS OF PUDDLES

ODES TO STINGING NETTLES

PHLEGM: A Pictorial Guide

CATS CRYING AT CHRISTMAS

HOW TO DROWN A WITCH IN FIVE EASY STEPS

A Dictionary of Non-existent Words

YE OLDE BOOKE OF
KNOCKE-KNOCKE JOKETHS

COOKING WITH
RARE BIRDS' EGGS

THE FOULEST SMELLS OF VICTORIAN LONDON:
A SCRATCH-AND-SNIFF BOOK

DISGUSTING DISEASES FOR DOGS

CAKE RECIPES OF RELIGIOUS MARTYRS:
IN LATIN

TEN THOUSAND TEDIOUS POEMS

THE Book of GROT

A SHORT HISTORY OF SOCKS

A LONG HISTORY
OF SOCKS

BEARDS OF THE BIBLE: A SPOTTER'S GUIDE

Chamberpots OF THE Rich and Famous

One by one, Mr and Mrs Meek pulled the books from the shelves. With just a candle to read by, they searched the millions upon millions of words for any reference to a **"FING"**. Just as they were about to lose all hope, Mr Meek thought he saw something move out of the corner of his eye.

"What was that?" he whispered.

"What was what?" she asked.

"Something moved."

"Maybe it was a rat? I hate rats."

With the candle, Mrs Meek illuminated a dingy corner of the vault. Indeed, something was moving underneath a pile of old newspapers.

RUSTLE! RUSTLE! RUSTLE!

She pushed her husband towards it to investigate further.

"Go on!"

"I am going! I am going!"

"Lift up the newspapers and see!" suggested Mrs Meek.

"No, after you."

"Oh, for goodness' sake! Let's not start all this again."

Reluctantly, Mr Meek lifted the old damp sheets of paper. To his surprise, all that was underneath was a book.

"It's a book!"

"Books can't move," she replied.

"This one did."

"What is it called?"

Mr Meek peered down to study the spine.

The title sent **chills** through him.

"It's called

THE
MONSTERPEDIA."

PART TWO

THE MONSTERPEDIA

Chapter 8

AN ENCYCLOPEDIA
OF MONSTERS

Mr and Mrs Meek set the book down on a rickety old table.

THUD.

THE MONSTERPEDIA was a huge leather-bound tome that must have been printed at least a few hundred years ago. It was, as the title

suggested, an encyclopedia of monsters. Mrs Meek blew dust off the cover and opened it.

Might this book hold a clue to the existence of a **"FING"**?

It was the Meeks' final hope.

The book was, as far as anyone knew, the only one of its kind in existence. Inside it was an alphabetical list of terrifying creatures that were either long extinct or assumed to be mythical, with lavish hand-painted illustrations of these creatures on the opposite page. Neither Mr nor Mrs Meek had seen or heard of any of them before.

First there was an

AAGADONGDONG:

a man-eating underground bird.

On the next page was a

BOOBOO:

a giant slug that leaves a poisonous trail of slime in its wake.

Then there was the

CRUNKLETOAD:

a reptile so ugly it can kill a man with a look.

D was for

DUMDUM:

a cross between a jellyfish and a warthog,

and, judging by the illustration, even more hideous than it sounds.

EEBINKIBONK: *an amphibious monkey found only in the deepest depths of the oceans.*

The next page was **F**. The Meeks took a collective breath, praying that they would find what they were looking for.

"**'FING'!**" exclaimed Mother.

"YES!"

"We did it!"

"I could kiss you!" said Father.

"Please don't. Not at work, darling. And the **LIBRARY** has a strict no-canoodling rule."

"Of course. How silly of me. Would you care to read out what it says?"

Mrs Meek cleared her throat and began:

FING:

MAMMAL

This, the most rarest of rare beasts, is found only in the deepest, darkest, jungliest jungle.

The appearance of the fing is that of a fur-covered sphere. The size of the beasts varies wildly. One moment they can be as small as a marble, the next as large as a hot-air balloon. Fings have one large eye in the centre, and a hole on either side. One hole is a mouth, the other is its (for want of a more polite expression) bottom. But nobody can be sure which hole is which, not even the fing itself, which has been known to try to feed using its bottom. Having no arms or legs, fings move around by rolling, or sometimes even bouncing. Strangely enough, a fing's favourite food is biscuits of the custard-cream variety. The fing beasts can devour a hundred in seconds, but they will eat almost anything and everything. Fings leave behind a trail of foul-smelling droppings, which can be as big, if not bigger, than the creature itself.

WARNING!
NEVER, EVER KEEP A FING IN YOUR HOUSE. THEY ARE THE WORLD'S WORST PETS.

Fings are greedy, bad-tempered and sometimes just plain rude. Because they can grow to epic proportions, they may not just eat you out of house and home, they may very well eat your home. Worst of all, they might even eat you.

DOOM AWAITS YOU.

After she had finished reading, they both pored over the picture. The **FING** was a peculiar-looking thing. The illustration, just as the words had described, showed a ball of brown fur with one eye between two dark holes.

"Oh dear," said Father.

"Oh dear indeed," agreed Mother. With that, she closed the book. "Well, that's the end of that, then. There is no way our darling daughter can have a **FING.**"

"Poor thing. She is going to be so bitterly disappointed," said Father.

"I know. Well, I think it best you break the bad news to her."

"Me?"

"Yes, Mr Meek! It's your turn."

"No, no, no," protested Mr Meek. "It is definitely your turn."

"Let's do it together," reasoned Mrs Meek.

"A splendid idea!"

"Thank you."

"You can go first."

Chapter 9
ROLLED IN RABBIT DROPPINGS

So, with heavy hearts, Mr and Mrs Meek picked up their daughter from school. Once again, I mean "picked up", literally. They picked Myrtle up and carried her all the way home, before depositing her as gently as they possibly could on the sofa.

THUMP!

Mr and Mrs Meek were trying to hide the worry they were feeling at breaking the bad news to their daughter, but it was daubed all over their faces.

"Perhaps you might like to play a game, Myrtle, my love," suggested Father. "Or do a jigsaw? Or watch the television?"

Distraction. Distraction. Distraction.

"CARTOONS!" demanded Myrtle.

"Here's the remote!" said Mother, handing her daughter the chocolate-stained black gadget.

Myrtle scowled back at her. "You press the button for me, you lazy old moo!"

Mrs Meek did what she was told, and a **CARTOON** flickered on to the television screen. Myrtle liked the violent ones the best, where animals ran into walls, fell off cliffs or simply exploded. Her favourite **CARTOON** series were:

With their daughter momentarily distracted by the sight of a cartoon rabbit being flattened by a steamroller, Mr Meek nodded to his wife. This was her cue. She scurried off to the kitchen. They had a secret plan. The pair hoped that if they gave their daughter the biggest slab of chocolate cake in history this would soften the blow of her not getting a **FING.**

The **CARTOON** finished, and as the theme music played Myrtle remembered what she had forgotten.

"Where's my **FING?**" she shouted.

"Cake! Cake! Cake!" yelped Father.

"Coming right up, Father!" replied Mrs Meek, staggering into the living room carrying a stupendous slab of cake. It was the size of a small garden shed. "There you go, Myrtle my angel," she said as she set it down on the coffee table.

THUD!

"Haven't you got a **bigger** slice?" demanded the girl.

"Sadly not," replied Mother. "It's bigger than the cake it came from."

This, of course, couldn't strictly be true, but it fooled Myrtle.

"It looks like delicious cake, my beautiful bunnykins. Do tuck in!" prompted Father.

Not being a regular user of cutlery, Myrtle simply leaned forward and buried her face in the cake. It was how a hog might enjoy its dinner.

GRIBBLE GROOBLE GRUBBLE!

Mother and Father sighed with relief. That feeling was sadly not to last. In no time at all, the girl had polished off the giant slab of cake. She lifted her head, her face now covered in chocolate icing.

"I want my **FING!**" she repeated, spraying her parents with chocolate-cake crumbs as she spoke.

Mr and Mrs Meek were covered from head to toe. It looked as if they had been rolled in rabbit droppings.

"Ah yes, yes, yes, yes, of course. The famous **FING...**" began Father, before losing his nerve.

"I will let your mother take over from here."

Mrs Meek shot a look at Mr Meek, most displeased. He was even meeker than she was. "Well, my sweet princess," she began. "Your father and I found this book deep in the vaults of the **LIBRARY**—"

"LISTEN!" growled the girl. "I want my **FING**. And I want it NOW!"

Things were going from bad to worse. The cake hadn't helped at all. If anything, it had given Myrtle a sugar rush that made her even more foul-tempered than usual.

"Well, er, you see, um…" the lady spluttered. "Father, you can take over from here."

"We, er, um, well…" he began, a look of terror now in his eyes.

"SPIT IT OUT!" bawled the girl.

"My cherub, we searched and searched every book in the **LIBRARY** to find out what a **FING** is."

"A **FING** is a **FING**. Duh!" mocked Myrtle.

"Quite. We found only one reference to it in the whole of the **LIBRARY** – in this dusty old book that we discovered down in the secret underground vaults. Here."

Father nodded to Mother, who lumbered over with the ancient tome.

"It's called **THE MONSTERPEDIA**," said Mrs Meek. "Have a look! It's fascinating reading."

Mother went to pass the book to her daughter, but the book actually pushed back.

"I HATE BOOKS! THEY MAKE MY BRAIN HURT!" Myrtle exclaimed, batting **THE MONSTERPEDIA** away with her hand.

THUMP!

The book slapped her back.

THWACK!

"OUCH!" screamed the girl. "Get that thing away from me!"

Mother took hold of the book. "Let me help you, sugar-plum fairy." Mother flicked through the dusty old book, and opened it at the right page.

"This, my rainbow child, is a **FING**. Have a read."

"You read it!" ordered Myrtle.

Mrs Meek proceeded to read aloud from the book, placing particular emphasis on this particular part:

WARNING!
NEVER, EVER KEEP A FING IN YOUR HOUSE.
THEY ARE THE WORLD'S WORST PETS.

"So, my dove of love?" prompted Mother. "What do you think? Surely, surely, surely, you don't want a **FING** now."

The pair looked longingly at their daughter, their hands glued together in prayer.

Chapter 10
AGHASTLIEST

"I fink," began Myrtle, her tongue tracing the plate for any uneaten crumbs, "having a **FING** as a pet would be a big, fat disaster."

Mr and Mrs Meek let out a humongous sigh of relief.

"HUH!"

Their lives had been spared.

"We couldn't agree more!" exclaimed Mother.

Father beamed. "You took the words right out of our mouths!"

"The creature would destroy everyfing!" Myrtle continued.

"You are so right! Righter than right!" cooed Mrs Meek.

"What a clever, clever girl you are!" agreed Mr Meek.

"The car. The house. **EVERYFING.** It might even kill us all!"

"Excellent point!" agreed Father.

"Yes, best not to die if you can possibly avoid it," echoed Mother.

"Who on earth would want a **FING** as a pet? Ha! Ha!" Myrtle laughed.

Her parents joined in.

"HO! HO! HO!"

"HEE! HEE! HEE!"

Even **THE MONSTERPEDIA** seemed to wobble around, chuckling silently to itself.

"ME!" replied Myrtle.

The laughter died. Instantly.

Mr and Mrs Meek couldn't believe their ears.

The book stopped dead still.

"I wanna **FING** as a pet."

"B-b-but—!" began Mother.

"NO BUTS!" shouted the girl, and she bashed her parents' heads together for emphasis.

CLONK!

"OW!"

"OUCH!"

"I said I wanna **FING.** And I want it NOW!"

Mr and Mrs Meek looked at each other, aghast. Both were so aghast it was impossible to tell who was the most aghast, or, to give it its improper word, aghastliest. You can decide for yourself by studying these two aghastliesque pictures…

For goodness' sake, don't take too long deciding. We have a story to be getting on with. Please let's agree that they were both extremely aghast. As indeed you'd be if you had to bring a **deadly animal** into your home.

Now all they had to do

was find one…

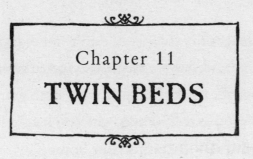

Chapter 11
TWIN BEDS

The big question was this... Who would have to go to the deepest, darkest, jungliest jungle in search of this blasted FING?

Sitting up in their twin beds, Mr and Mrs Meek discussed this, way into the night. Of course, both were desperate not to go, but, being who they were, the argument was remarkably polite.

"But you need a jolly good holiday, Father," began Mother with a smile. "You have been working so hard at the LIBRARY – you should go."

"No, no, no, you have always said you wanted to travel and explore the world, Mother," replied Father.

"Have I?"

"You said you wanted to go to the seaside."

"For the day!"

"Well, this will be very much like a day out at the seaside!"

"In what way?" pressed Mrs Meek.

Well, that stumped Mr Meek rather. "There might be an ice-cream van?" he offered pitifully.

"AN ICE-CREAM VAN!" Mrs Meek was incredulous. "In the deepest, darkest, jungliest jungle!"

There was a loud banging on the wall.

BOOM!

BOOM!

BOOM!

"KEEP IT DOWN IN THERE!" shouted Myrtle from her bedroom next door. "I can barely hear myself grunt!"

pFFFFFFT!

The grunt was so loud the whole house **rumbled**.

Needless to say, Mr and Mrs Meek both looked appalled.

Mother suddenly had a thought, and whispered to her husband, "Of course, one of us is going to have to stay behind and look after our darling daughter all on their own."

"I'll go!" he replied as quick as a flash.

"To the **deepest, darkest, jungliest jungle?**"

"Yes. So that's settled, then! Goodnight!"

With that, he switched off the light.

FLICK!

Mr Meek slept like a baby that night. He woke up every two hours, crying his eyes out.

Chapter 12
SOME LIGHT READING

At dawn the next morning, Mr Meek set off on his quest to find a **FING**. He had cast aside his bookish persona, and had now turned himself into an adventurer. Well, sort of. The man had put bicycle clips over the bottom of his trousers, in case he snagged them on some undergrowth.

Poor Mrs Meek was very tearful at the doorstep. Since the day they were married, the pair of librarian *lovebirds* had never spent a single night apart.

"Please, please be careful, Father," implored Mrs Meek.

Mr Meek was trying to be brave, though it was not his strong suit. "Don't you worry,

SPOT THE DIFFERENCE

NORMAL
MR MEEK

MR MEEK
THE ADVENTURER

Mother. I will be back with a **FING** before you know it. What's the absolute worst that could happen?"

"You could get eaten!" called Myrtle from an upstairs window.

"Thank you for your contribution, my angel sent from heaven," called Father. He smiled weakly at his wife. "I will do my absolute best not to."

"PROMISE!" she implored.

"I promise."

They kissed awkwardly. Their kisses were always awkward. Either their noses knocked, or chins bumped, or glasses crunched. Today their foreheads clunked together.

C L U N K !

"Ouch!"

"Argh!"

"Sorry."

"Sorry."

Mr Meek picked up his suitcase, took a deep breath and walked down the path.

"I miss you already!" called out Mrs Meek.

"Yuckety yuck, yuck, yuck!"

came the cry from upstairs.

Mr Meek blew a kiss back to his wife, which, fumbling, she caught.

"MOVE YOUR BOTTOM!"

shouted Myrtle.

Father picked up the pace, and with his suitcase in hand began walking to the bus stop. In his socks and sandals, shirt, tie, slacks and tweed blazer, he looked nothing like a jungle explorer. Having never left his local town before, he was woefully unprepared.

The only food he'd brought was a packed lunch that Mother had made him.

It consisted of:

1. A bread sandwich *(Father didn't like fillings as they were distracting)*

2. A packet of flavourless crisps *(no flavours, please, thank you kindly)*

3. A plain yoghurt *(just as he liked them)*

As is often the way with packed lunches, Father had scoffed the lot within five minutes of setting off from home, sitting on the bus to the airport. Soon after, he became cataclysmically hungry, and resorted to eating the plastic box in which his lunch had been packed. He ended up rather liking the taste, as there was none.

In his suitcase, Mr Meek had packed an anorak in case of rain, and spare pairs of underpants and socks. He'd also brought some light reading, a small selection of his favourite books from home:

A History of Cauliflower
Boring Buildings of Britain
Ponds
A Closer Look at Gravel
Tissues Around the World

One Hundred and One Poems About Leaves
A Spotter's Guide to Sandals
Church Pews Through the Ages
A Million Times Tables
Light Bulbs, Light Bulbs and More Light Bulbs

Plus he had taken out of the **LIBRARY** the book that had led him on this quest, **THE MONSTERPEDIA**. It was wriggling around in his suitcase. He just had to remember to return it within two weeks or there would be a hefty fine to pay.

Of course, Mr Meek had made some room for the most important items of all, the special **FING**-capturing equipment.

First, a rusty old hamster's cage that he'd found up in the loft, into which to put the **FING.**

Second, a giant tin of the **FING'S** favourite food, *custard-cream* biscuits. These were to lay a trail to tempt the **FING** into the hamster's cage as soon as he had spotted one.

Mr Meek's plan really was that simple.

How could it possibly go

wrong?

PART THREE

DEEPEST, DARKEST, JUNGLIEST JUNGLE

Chapter 13

UNDERPANTS
AND SOCKS

Mr Meek's journey to the **deepest, darkest, jungliest jungle** was long. When I say long, I mean looooooooooooooong.

It involved a plane,

a train,

a ship,

roller-skates,

a toboggan,

a donkey,

a canoe,

a camel,

a bicycle,

a hang-glider,

another donkey,

a hot-air balloon

and a rather
peeved-looking*
emu.

* *Peeved because emus do not like being ridden. At all. Do not try it. It will only end in tears. Yours, not the emu's.*

After a month (he really should have packed more underpants and socks as they were now only being changed weekly), Father looked a state. His glasses had **cracked**, he had grown a long, straggly beard, his clothes were torn into rags and, horror upon horror, he had lost one of his sandals.*

Worst of all, **THE MONSTERPEDIA** book was now overdue, and there was already a substantial fine of (10p) to pay. However, however, however, none of that really mattered as Mr Meek had finally reached his destination. The deepest, darkest, jungliest jungle.

HOME OF THE FING!

In case you are wondering where the deepest, darkest, jungliest jungle is, and might be suspecting I have simply made it up,** please peruse the map over the page.

---

* *Said sandal had been devoured by an emu.*
** *How dare you!*

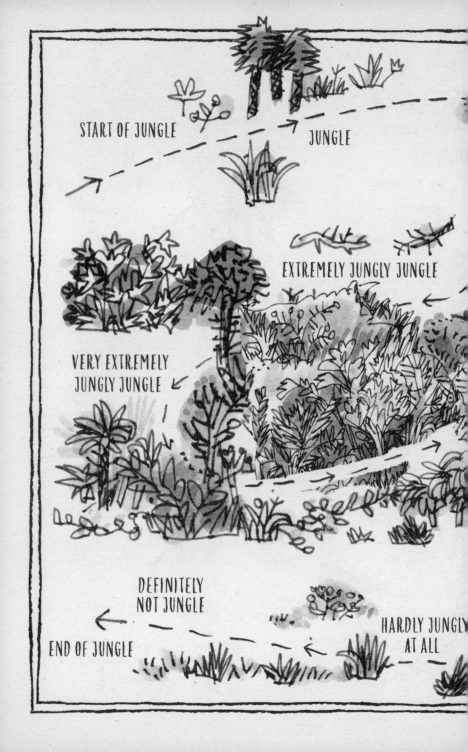

Now that he was in the deepest, darkest, jungliest jungle, Mr Meek had to find a FING.

The problem was
he couldn't spot one
anywhere.

So Mr Meek climbed up the tallest tree he could find. Holding on tight to **THE MONSTERPEDIA**, which was trying to squirm out of his hand, he spotted a number of creatures from the pages of the book.

There was:

The **wong-wing bird.** It is a one-winged (or uni-winged) bird, which is unsurprisingly flightless. It leaps confidently off branches of trees before plummeting to the ground.

SPLAT!

SPLAT!

SPLAT!

A **honkopotamus**. This is a distant relation of the hippopotamus, but the **honkopotamus** is legless (not drunk – it has no legs). As a consequence, the honkopotamus moves around by honking. The force of the wind being pushed

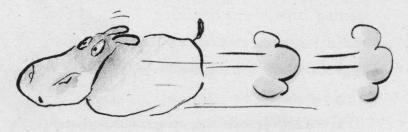

out of the back blowhole is so powerful it works like a jet engine. Despite its size and weight, the **honkopotamus** has been known to reach speeds of over a hundred miles an hour. Whoosh!

 The mingo. A miniature mungo.

The mungo. A giant mingo.

The **pludge.** This is a venomous giant worm, half red, half white. A **pludge** is too large for the holes into which it burrows and ends up getting stuck. Hence one half gets sunburned and turns red, while the other stays underground and remains white.

SIZZLE!

The **flattened humming bungbung.** This hairless rodent hums tunelessly all day and night.

"Pom pom
pom pom
pom!"

The humming is so wretched it makes the ears of any listeners bleed. As a result, the **bungbung** often finds itself being sat on by bigger creatures desperate to make it stop.

S Q U I S H !

A **purplephant.** This is a species of elephant that hangs upside down from branches by its trunk. It stays there for so long that it turns purple. If you are walking under one when it turns purple, beware: that means it is going to drop to the ground and flatten you in a second.

DOOF!

A **lood.** Not to be confused with a loooo**d**, a **lood** is a lime-green lizard so terrifying-looking that it is scared of itself. If it sees its own reflection in the water, it desperately swims away, sometimes for hundreds of miles.

"ARGH!"

A loooood. Not to be confused with a **lood.** This is a hairless white ape, which is so embarrassed about being naked that it crosses its legs and hops around everywhere.

SKIP!

H O P !

Also known as "the nude loooood" or "the hopping loooood" or "the nude hopping loooood". One was once spotted shoplifting dresses from a womenswear boutique, causing the old dear behind the counter to faint.

DOINK!

However, despite Mr Meek being able to see for miles around from the top of the tree, there was absolutely no sign of a **FING** anywhere. The wind blew across the deepest, darkest, jungliest jungle, and his thoughts turned to his darling daughter. As a father, he couldn't let Myrtle down. He had to find a **FING,** whatever it took. If not, there would be tears. Most likely his, not hers. He thought about home. While the sun was setting across the jungle, Mr Meek pictured Mrs Meek putting Myrtle to bed. Right about now, his wife would be reading their daughter a bedtime story before being clonked on the head with the book and fleeing from the girl's bedroom, screaming.

"ARGH!"

A tear rolled down Father's cheek. It was a beautiful scene.

"Myrtle," he said, "I won't let you down."

Now lost in thought, he lost his footing. It was hard gripping on to a tree with just the one

sandal. As a result, he slid down
the trunk at speed, his bottom
hitting each and every branch
as he descended…

DOINK!

"OOF!"

DOINK!

"OOF!"

DOINK! "OOF!"

DOINK! "OOF!"

"OOF!"

DOINK!

DOINK! "OOF!"

DOINK! "OOF!"

"OOF!"

DOINK!

"OOF!"

…before he hit the
ground with a **THUD!**

"OOOOOOOOOOOFFFFF!"

Suddenly Mr Meek remembered he had lost his hold on the book. **"THE MONSTERPEDIA!"** he exclaimed.

Right on cue, the mighty tome thwacked him on the head.

CLONK!

It knocked him out cold.

Chapter 15
TRAP!

Father woke up as **THE MONSTERPEDIA** bonked him on the head.

Mr Meek grabbed hold of the book. Unsure of where to put it, he stuffed it down the back of his trousers. Needless to say, the book didn't

like that one bit, and tried
to squirm out.

"STOP!" ordered Mr
Meek, giving it a light slap.
Anyone who was there might
have thought here was a man
who was slapping his own
bottom. Fortunately for Mr Meek, he was all
alone in the **deepest, darkest, jungliest jungle.**

At once, the man began making a plan. If he
was going to catch a **FING**, he would have to
set a trap. So Mr Meek found a clearing in the

deepest, darkest, jungliest jungle not much bigger than a paddling pool. First, he opened his now rather battered suitcase, and took out the tin of **custard creams.** It was heavy as it contained one hundred biscuits. He set the tin down next to his feet. Then he took out the hamster's cage and put it on the jungle floor. As quietly as he could, he opened the little door of the cage.

CREAK!

 The plan was to lay a trail of **custard creams,** with the last one actually inside the cage. All the man would have to do was wait until a **FING** followed the trail of biscuits. Then, as soon as it was nibbling the final one inside the cage, Father would slam the door, and BINGO!* The **FING** would be trapped.

---

* Or, as we are in the jungle, we could say BONGO!

RUSTLE RUSTLE RUSTLE...

A sound came from the bushes.

"Is anyone there?" called out Mr Meek.

There was no reply. Not that a wild animal, or indeed any animal, was likely to call back,

"Yes, I am here, woohoo!" "HELLOOOO!"

The silence that followed put the man's mind at rest.

"Probably just another gust of wind," he muttered to himself.

Of course, Mr Meek had exercised incredible restraint in not gobbling down all the *custard creams* himself. It had been a month since he'd set off from home with only a small packed lunch. At one point, he'd become so ravenous that he'd resorted to eating a pair of his own UNDERPANTS. Dirty ones at that. Needless to say, they didn't taste good. Savoury rather than sweet.*

---

* *Whatever you do in life, do not try to eat your own underwear. Even smothered in tomato ketchup, it will taste bad.*

Father knew he couldn't fail his daughter. There would be hell to pay if he didn't return home with a **FING.** Goodness knows what hideous humiliation she would devise for him this time. Previously when Mr Meek had displeased his daughter she had...

...made Father sit on the naughty step outside in the snow until his bum went completely numb with cold...

...sent him to bed before he'd even got up...

...buried all his clothes in the garden so he had to go to work in the **LIBRARY** wearing only his vest and pants...

...buried Mother in the flowerbed...

...forced Father to eat cold cabbage for breakfast, lunch and dinner...

...told him to stand in a corner. On one leg. Balancing a plant pot on his head. For a year...

...set him to work scrubbing the house from top to bottom, armed only with his toothbrush...

...then made him clean his teeth with that toothbrush...

...made him sleep in the shed...

...and ordered him to drink from a puddle.

When Father turned back to open the biscuit tin, he was horrified to find the lid was already off and it was completely empty.

"NOOO!" he cried.

This was a DISASTER! Someone or **something** had eaten all the *custard creams*!*

---

* *I know what you are thinking, but, no, it wasn't me.*

Chapter 16
SUSPICIOUS DROPPINGS

Who was the phantom *custard-cream* thief? There may have been no *custard-cream* biscuits left in the tin, but there was a suspicious trail of steaming droppings leading from it. Droppings that looked strangely custardy and creamy.*

The droppings led all the way from the clearing, through some very jungly parts of the deepest, darkest, jungliest jungle to the mouth of a cave.

Mr Meek grimaced. "Oh no."

He was afraid of the dark. Going down into the vaults of the **LIBRARY** was bad enough, but this was infinitely more terrifying. There was a long list of things that gave him THE WILLIES.

---

* *Although not at all tasty.*

THINGS THAT GIVE MR MEEK THE WILLIES:

Washing-up gloves

Brussels sprouts

Vending machines

Whisks

Umbrellas

Clowns

Brown bananas

Stairlifts

Pips

Coffee-flavoured chocolates

Darts players

Balloon animals

Bubble wrap

Lampshades

Walk-in baths

Liquorice

Men with hairy toes

Women with hairy toes

Anyone with the name Colin

Lists

Keeping in mind his daughter's fury if he didn't return home with a **FING,** Mr Meek took a deep breath, and stepped inside the dark, damp cave.

His footsteps echoed in the blackness.

SHONT SHONT SHONT...

"HELLO!" he called out.

"HELLO!" a voice came back.

The man was spooked out of his skin. To hide his fear, Mr Meek put on his bravest, boomiest voice.

"Who's there?" he demanded.

"WHO'S THERE?" was the defiant reply.

"I asked first."

"I ASKED FIRST."

"No, you didn't. I did."

"NO, YOU DIDN'T. I DID."

"You are being ridiculous!" he shouted into the darkness.

"YOU ARE BEING RIDICULOUS," came the reply.

"No, I am not."

"NO, I AM NOT."

"Yes, you are."

"YES, YOU ARE."

"Show yourself!"

"SHOW YOURSELF!"

"You go first!"

"YOU GO FIRST!"

"Stop repeating everything I say."

"STOP REPEATING EVERYTHING I SAY."

"Hang on…"

"HANG ON…"

"Am I talking to my own echo?"

There was silence for a moment, before Mr Meek's voice bounced back. **"YES."**

Now he was seriously spooked.

Father fumbled in what was left of his pocket for a box of matches. Trembling, he lit one.

STRIKE!

FIZZ!

With the flicker of light from the match, he searched out the darkest corners of the cave.

Something was moving.

Something small.

Something furry.

Something
FINGY...

Chapter 17

WIGGLED, WAGGLED AND WOGGLED

When the light illuminated whatever it was moving around in the shadows, it let out a low growl.

"GRRR!"

Like most people, Mr Meek thought of himself as someone who was good with animals, even though he'd once been bitten on the bottom by a horse. A pantomime horse. Thinking he could tame this creature, he tiptoed forward and crouched down. Striking another match...

STRIKE!

WHIZZ!

...he had his first good look at it.

BINGO!

Or, rather, BONGO!

This thing was indeed a **FING.** It was exactly as **THE MONSTERPEDIA** had described. The creature was no bigger than a tennis ball. It was round and furry, and moved about by rolling.

Two little holes were visible, one on either side of a large eye, which swivelled round to look at Mr Meek. One hole must be its mouth, and the other its bottom. However, despite these two holes performing wildly different functions, they were completely indistinguishable from each other.

Inexplicably, Mr Meek began speaking to it in a baby voice. As if an animal were more likely to understand you if you spoke to it as if you still wore nappies.

"Hello, little thing, or should I say **'FING'**! Do you want to come home with me?" cooed Mr Meek.

"**GRRR!**" came the reply.

Despite this not sounding anything like a yes, he reached out his hand to stroke the animal. This proved to be a mistake.

A big mistake.

Enormous.

Gargantuan.

Humongous.

Let's just agree it was big.

"**GRRRR!**"

SNAP!

"**ARGH!**" screamed Father.

This **FING** had bitten on to his index finger. And it wasn't letting go. The pain was eye-watering.

"YEOW!"

Mr Meek's face had turned scarlet, and his hair was standing up on end.

"MINGY! MINGY! MOO!"*

The man wiggled and waggled and woggled his finger as hard as he could.

"GET OFF ME!"

---

* Well, *you might say this if you were in that much pain.*

The creature just sank its teeth in deeper. Its eye narrowed. It was as if it were going in for the kill.

"NaNaNaNaNaNaNaNaNaNaNaNaNaNaNaNaNaNaNaNaNaNaNaNa!"*

Next, Mr Meek hobbled across the cave, and tried to whack the creature off him on the stone entrance.

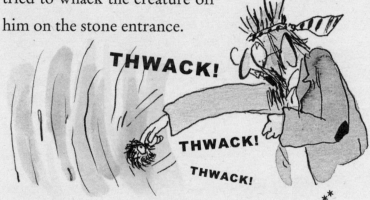

THWACK!

THWACK!

THWACK!

Still the creature sank its teeth deeper and deeper into the man's finger.

"GOGOGOGOGOGOGOGOoooooooooooooOOOOOOOOOOOOOO!"**
WATER!" he exclaimed. "I bet it hates water!"

---

* *Another scream of pain, in case you were wondering.*
** *A scream, of course. Keep up.*

As fast as he could, Mr Meek staggered towards a lake. Without thinking what might be in there (this was the **deepest, darkest, jungliest jungle**, remember) he leaped in.

SPLOSH!

To his surprise, Mr Meek could stand. Up to his armpits in water, he began giving the **FING** an ultimatum.

"Right! That's it! That's really it! I need my finger back! It's one of my favourites. I need it for all kinds of things: turning the pages of a book, scratching my bottom, picking my nose!*

---

* *Best not done consecutively.*

I am sorry, **FING,** but you give me no choice!"

With that, the man took charge. Finally, he found the **hero** he'd always thought might just be lurking beneath his meek exterior. At last he was the most manliest man in the whole of mandom. YES!

He lifted his finger high in the air to savour the moment, before plunging it deep under the water.

SPLISH!

Mr Meek held it under, sure that the **FING** would release its grip.

Smiling to himself, he waited. And waited. And waited. And waited some more.

Then the *strangest* thing happened.

Bubbles began floating to the surface.

BLUB! BLUB! BLUB!

The bubbles were huge, brown and foul-smelling. Eye-wateringly, nose-ticklingly, stomach-turningly stinky. In a word, **pongywongywoowah.** *

It was a very different stench from the creamy, custardy droppings. Mr Meek held his breath and peered down into the dark water. His feet weren't touching the lake bed after all. They were touching something big and grey and alive.

BLUB! BLUB! BLUB!

---

* *Another real word you will find in*
The Walliamsictionary.

Still more lethal-smelling bubbles burst on the surface.

It was only then that Mr Meek realised that he was, in fact, standing on an animal.

Not just any animal.

Oh no.

A **honkopotamus!**

Chapter 18
DOUBLE TROUBLE

Now, of course, the important thing to remember with **honkopotamuses** (or, rather, **honkopotami** for the plural*) is that a bubble is just the beginning. A bubble means there is a lot more to come. Mr Meek looked down to see a huge jet of air shooting out from between his feet.

PFT!

The creature powered through the water like a torpedo.

PFFFFT!

WHOOSH!

---

* As you can tell, complete and utter accuracy is of paramount importance in this book.

Despite hitting a hundred miles an hour, the **FING** was still not letting go of Father's finger.

"WINKY WINKY WOO-WAH!"

If you thought things couldn't get any worse, then think again. In fright at all the commotion, a flock of **wong-wing** birds took off from a tree in which they'd been nesting.

CLUCK! CLUCK! CLUCK!

Having just one wing (each, not between them – that would be plain silly), they spun through the air, whacking the poor man across the face…

THWACK! THWACK! THWACK!

"OW! OW! OW!"

…before they nose-dived into the water.

SPLISH! SPLASH! SPLOSH!

This served to continue the chain reaction. The **wong-wing** birds plunging into the lake attracted the attention of another creature lurking in the depths.

The two-headed **croco-croco**.

It also had its own entry in **THE MONSTERPEDIA**. The **croco-croco** was not unlike a crocodile, but instead of having a head and a tail it had two heads and no tail.*

Two huge, hungry mouths to feed meant DOUBLE TROUBLE.

The main drawback of having two heads and no tail was that the creature was directionless. One head wanted to go one way, and the other, well, the other way. Still, Mr Meek looked like a tasty treat to this creature. So the **croco-croco** thrashed around in pursuit, both sets of jaws snapping at the man as if he were dinner.

SNAP! SNAP! SNAP!

---

* *Two tails and no head would be worse.*

What with the **FING** biting his finger, the **honkopotamus** blasting bottom bubbles from below, the **wong-wing** birds dive-bombing from above and of course the **croco-croco** snapping at his heels, Mr Meek was beginning to think that this might be the end.

"HEEEEEEELLLP!" he cried. "PLEASE CAN SOMEONE TAKE **THE MONSTERPEDIA** BOOK BACK TO THE **LIBRARY?** THERE IS A FEE TO PAY!"

Shouting didn't help one bit. In fact, it made things worse. Much worse. The shout woke up another animal. Not just any animal. Oh no. Mr Meek had woken up the **deadliest animal** in the world.

Chapter 19
FLYING SAUSAGE

No, the **deadliest animal** in the world was not Myrtle.

But as Mr Meek was racing towards certain doom his thoughts did flash to his daughter. In his mind's eye, he wanted to conjure up a pretty picture of her before he died, although, however hard he tried, he just couldn't find an image of Myrtle doing anything remotely nice. Myrtle didn't do nice. But she was very good at "nasty". All kinds of images flooded into Mr Meek's mind...

Myrtle snapping the Christmas tree in half when she didn't get enough presents.

CRUNCH!

Myrtle stamping on the Snakes and Ladders board when she was losing the game. **STOMP!**

Myrtle shoving her entire birthday cake into her gob in one go so no one else could have a piece. G U R G L E !

Myrtle punching a hole through the television set when her favourite **CARTOON** ended. **THUMP!**

Myrtle cheating on school sports day by making her mother drive her round the racetrack. **BRUM!** *"FASTER! FASTER!"*

Myrtle deliberately flooding the entire house when asked to hurry up in the bath. **SPLOSH!**

Myrtle eating all her mother and father's books when they encouraged her to read one. **M U N C H !**

Myrtle holding her headmaster upside down and giving him a bogwash when she was given a detention for giving her teacher a bogwash. *FLUSH!*

Myrtle setting up a stall outside the house to sell every single one of her parents' possessions so she could buy herself a roller coaster.

KERCHING!

Myrtle wailing so much for a Mr Whippy that the ice-cream van actually toppled over on to its side.

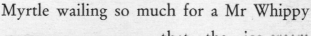

THUNK!

No. The **deadliest animal** in the world is not Myrtle.
It is a helephant.

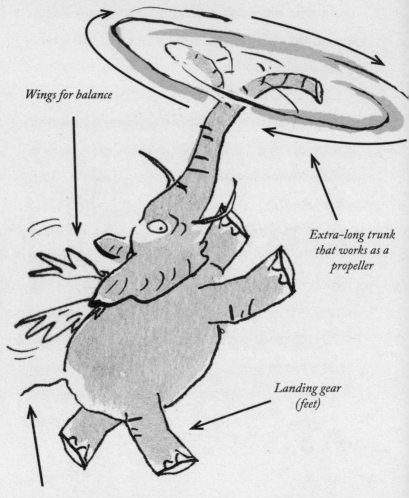

Wings for balance

Extra-long trunk that works as a propeller

Landing gear (feet)

Tail or rudder for steering left and right

This is, quite simply, a flying elephant.

How does it fly?

With its trunk, of course. I thought that would be obvious.

If you had studied **THE MONSTERPEDIA**, you would know.

The **helephant's** trunk is unusually long. When the animal spins it round fast enough, it works exactly like a propeller.

What could be more dangerous than a flying elephant?

Nothing. If it crash-lands on you, you are jam.

On hearing Father's shout, the **helephant** woke up with a "**h a r r u m p h**" from the riverbank where it was **s l u m b e r i n g**. **Helephants** always wake up with a "**h a r r u m p h**", because, however much sleep they have, it is never enough.*

On being woken up, the animal wanted revenge. So, with a spin of its trunk, it took to the sky.

---

* *Once a helephant slept for seventeen years, and still woke up in a foul mood.*

BUZZ!

How does a helephant steer?

With its tail, of course.

The tail works as a rudder.

Come on, this couldn't be more straight-forward.

Mr Meek heard a loud buzzing from above. A shadow passed over him. He looked up and saw a huge, fat flying sausage soaring through the sky, blotting out the sun.

"Oh…"

But before Mr Meek could say "cripes" the **helephant** hooked him up by his trousers with one of its tusks, giving him a nasty wedgie.*

---

* *No wedgies are nice, but, even by the standards of nasty wedgies, this was a particularly vicious one.*

"SHONTISISIMO!" cried Mr Meek as he was plucked from the back of the **honkopotamus** and whisked up into the air.

THE MONSTERPEDIA wriggled around in the back of his trousers in an attempt to escape. Meanwhile, the **FING** simply bit harder on to his finger, closing its one eye in concentration.

"BOOM DITTY BOOM DITTY BOOM BOOM!"

The pain was indescribable, so I won't even try, other than to call it indescribable.

"LET ME GO!" screamed Mr Meek to the helephant.

Then he looked below him. It was a long way down.

"ACTUALLY, KEEP HOLDING ON TO ME, PLEASE! THANK YOU SO MUCH!"

Chapter 20
FURRY FINGER-WARMER

With its trunk whirring like a propeller, the **helephant** soared above the clouds. It was bitterly cold all the way up there where the sky meets outer space. Mr Meek found himself covered in a light dusting of ice, like a lolly fresh out of the freezer. He looked

down at his finger. To his unsurprise,* the **FING** was still very much attached to it. Its one eye was blinking due to the cold.

Despite the pain, which as previously described was indescribable, it was at least the one part of Mr Meek's body that was not freezing. The **FING** was a furry finger-warmer. The only problem was that you couldn't take it off.

Now hundreds of miles from where it lived, the helephant was ready to take revenge and drop its load. In an instant, Mr Meek's trousers became unhooked from the tusk.

"ARGH!" he screamed as he tumbled through the sky.

WHIZZ!

"HOOBY! HOOBY!" cried the helephant.

---

* *Yes, that is a real word too, clever clogs. Just check your* **Walliamsictionary.**

If Mr Meek didn't act fast, he would be nothing more than a splattering of Bolognese sauce on the ground.

If only he had a parachute!

Mr Meek looked at the round furry thing still attached to his finger.

DING!

He had an idea. An idea so utterly preposterous that it might just work.

According to **THE MONSTERPEDIA**, **FINGS** could vary dramatically in size. Sometimes they were as small as a marble, other times the size of a hot-air balloon.

With this in mind, as Mr Meek was plummeting towards the ground…

WHIZZ!

...he began blowing air into the other end of the **FING** as quickly as he could.

PUFF!

PUFF!

PUFF!

The **FING'S** eye flickered. Whatever was the man doing?

Just like a Lilo, the creature began to inflate. Soon it was the size of a football, then a beach ball, and then Mr Meek used every last bit of puff he had.

PUUUUUUUFFFFFFFFFFF!

The **FING** was now a hundred times or more its original size. Not only was it as big as a hot-air balloon, it worked like one too. Now, instead of falling, Mr Meek was floating up, up and away.

S W I S H !

"I AM FLYING!"

he exclaimed.

Chapter 21
HOT-AIR
FING-ING

Now all Mr Meek had to do was steer a course home. As he saw the continents roll by hundreds of miles beneath him, he thought happily about all the money he was saving on airfares. Using his leg as a rudder, Mr Meek steered a course over Africa, across mainland

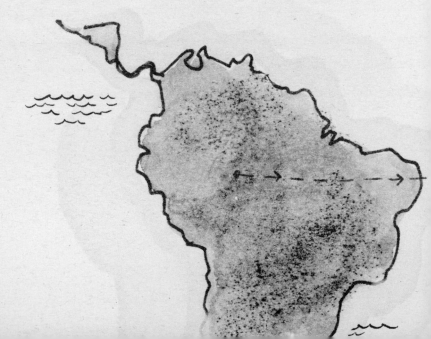

Europe to the British Isles. Every
now and again, he would blow
more air into the **FING'S**
end to stop it from
deflating.

PFFFT!

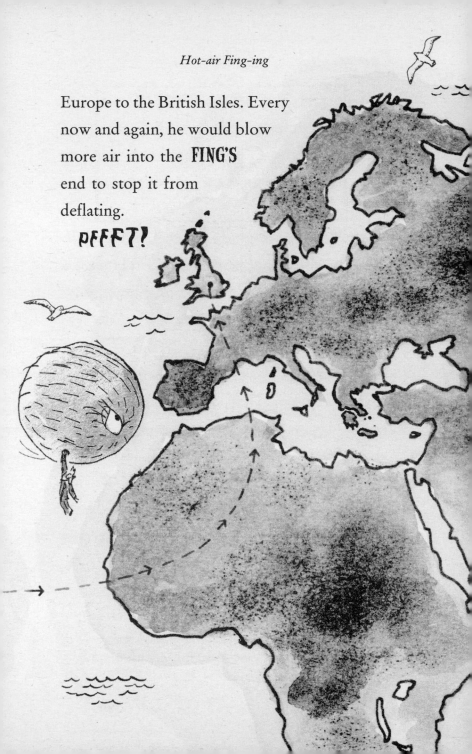

Best of all, **THE MONSTERPEDIA** was still tucked safely down the back of his trousers, and even though there was an overdue fine to pay there could have been a much heftier one for a lost book.

Mr Meek was mightily pleased with himself. If he could have, he would've given himself a pat on the back. He'd invented a brand-new mode of travel.

Hot-air **FING**-ing.*

In a matter of days, Mr Meek was floating over his town. Then his street. Then his house.

A smug look spread across his face. What a super surprise he had for his darling daughter. Not only had he cheated death, but he had brought her the greatest present of all.

---

* This is a variation of hot-air ballooning. Hot-air ballooning is not to be confused with hot-air babooning. That is when baboons talk absolute nonsense for hours on end.

Something of myth. Something of legend. Something from another world. Some **FING.**

"I've done it!" hollered Father. "Little old me!"

He reached up to the furry ball to embrace it. "Thank you! Thank you! Thank you! For never letting go! For letting me blow air into your wotsit!"

Unfortunately, the man squeezed too hard on the **FING.** Its one eye widened in shock. Just like a balloon, the air spluttered out infinitely faster than you could put it in.

PFFFFFFFT!

WHIZZZZ!

Mr Meek had been heading for his garden, looking forward to a nice, gentle landing on the lawn. He was not going to make it. Now he was heading straight for the house.

"NOOO!" he screamed.

Father was going too fast.

He crashed through the roof.

KABAM!

BOO-BOOM!

He smashed through the first floor before landing in a dusty heap on the living-room carpet.

"OOF!"

Fortunately, **THE MONSTERPEDIA**, which was still down the back of his trousers, cushioned the fall. If not, he might very well have suffered from a broken bottom.*

"Please remind me to take that back to the **LIBRARY**," said Mr Meek. "There is a fine to pay."

---

* *Not something for which you want to be admitted to hospital.*

"Doctor, Doctor, it's my bottom. I fear it may be broken."

"Just let me see… Oh, this is embarrassing… Yes, it is broken. We are going to have to put a cast on it for the next month or so."

"What if I need the toilet?"

"I'm afraid you will just have to hold it in."

"YIPES!"

Chapter 22
BEARD DOWN TO HIS BELLY BUTTON

"**Y**ou took your time!" announced Myrtle, who was slumped on the sofa, watching **CARTOONS.**

"Oh, my goodness me, are you all right, dearest?" yelled a worried Mrs Meek as she rushed into the room.

"Yeah. I'm fine!" replied the girl.

"No! Not you, my heavenly angel! I meant Father!" Just one look at him was enough to make Mother burst into a river of tears. "Boo! Hoo! Hoo! Poor, poor you!"

It was true Mr Meek did not look his best. The man of the house had been gone for months. Now he was as skinny as a rake and his beard reached down to his belly button. Since he'd thundered through the roof and ceiling of the living room, he was plastered from head to toe with dust. The most striking thing of all was that, unbelievably, he still had a furry ball stuck to the end of his finger, even though it had now deflated back to its usual size.

"Please don't cry, Mother," said Father as he wobbled to his feet, "for this is a happy day. Behold!" Slowly, he lifted his finger into the air. "Look what I have for our darling daughter!"

Mrs Meek looked on in awe at this new heroic Mr Meek. Now she was crying tears of pride.

"Yes!" continued Mr Meek.

"Your father has successfully completed his deadly mission. All the way from the deepest, darkest, jungliest jungle, I bring you this! A **FING!**"

Myrtle looked away from the television set for a moment and glanced at it, before uttering,

"I already got one!"

PART FOUR

BIG FING
AND
LITTLE FING

Chapter 23

HOW WE LAUGHED

Needless to say, Mr Meek could not believe his ears. "What do you mean, 'I already got **one!**'?"

"A **FING,** stupid!" said Myrtle. "I already got a **FING.**" The girl pointed to a little cage in the corner of the room. "Look, dummy!"

In a state of shock, Father paced over, and peered through the bars. There, nestling in some torn-up newspaper, was indeed a **FING,** blinking with its one little eye.

"Where on earth did you get this from?" he spluttered.

"Pet shop."

"PET SHOP?"

"Yeah! Are you deaf? I just said that!"

Father looked over to Mother, who nodded her head.

"I am so, so sorry, darling," began Mother, her face still wet with tears, "but you'd been gone so long that with a heavy heart I'd all but given up hope of you ever returning."

"We thought you'd snuffed it," added Myrtle.

"CHARMING!" replied Father.

"So I thought there was no harm in seeing if I could get a **FING** from somewhere. Especially as Myrtle began… How can I put this politely? She began *kicking off.*"

"I gave Mum a bogwash," chuckled Myrtle.

"My hair needed washing anyway. And would you believe it?" continued Mother, wincing at the memory. "It turned out they had a **FING** for sale at the local pet shop! Oh, how we laughed!"

"HA! HA! HA!" agreed the girl.

Mr Meek took a deep breath. He wasn't one

to get angry, but he certainly felt peeved.*

"I've travelled thousands of miles," spluttered Father, "very nearly been eaten alive, and there was a **FING** in the **local pet shop** all along?"

"I am so sorry, dear," replied Mrs Meek. "I suppose we should have checked before you set off. The **FING** was actually on special offer."

"SPECIAL OFFER?"

"Yes! Half price. So that was a boon."

---

* The gradations of anger are as follows:

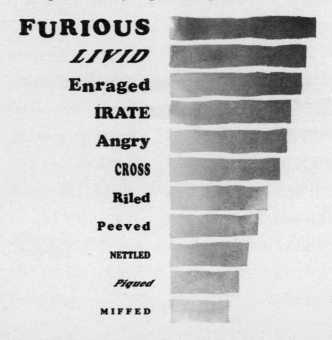

FURIOUS
LIVID
Enraged
IRATE
Angry
CROSS
Riled
Peeved
NETTLED
Piqued
MIFFED

Father looked as if he were about to burst into tears. He slumped down in what was left of his armchair.

"Ouch!"

Mr Meek still had **THE MONSTERPEDIA** stuffed down the back of his trousers. The book was now wriggling like crazy to

escape from being right next to the bottom of a man who'd not had a bath for months. As soon as Father pulled the back of his trousers open,

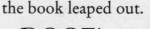

the book leaped out.

DOOF!

It landed on what was left of the coffee table.

Its leather cover now had buttock imprints on it.

Mr Meek looked down at his finger. Despite everything, the **FING** was still attached to it, and looking up at him with hate in its one eye. Then the strangest thing happened. The man began to laugh. "Ha! Ha! Ha!"

It wasn't a laugh you hear when something's funny. It was a laugh that made you think he'd gone bananas.*

"Now we have two **FINGS!** Two! Two! Two of the world's worst pet. TWO! Ha! Ha! Ha!"

---

* *Or, to use the correct term, "crazy in the coconut".*

"Yeah," said Myrtle. "I already got one. I don't want another one."

"Don't be impolite to your father, my perfect angel," prompted Mother.

"Shut your cake hole!" snapped the girl.

Mrs Meek fell silent.

"Take it," pleaded Father as he held up his **FINGY** finger. "Please. I beg you!"

"NO!" she barked. **"FINGS** are dead boring!"

"Boring?"

"Yeah. They don't do nuffink. I thought it was gonna destroy the whole house, but instead it just rolls around like a fat, furry egg."

Mr Meek was defeated. "Then please, please can someone at least help me get this blasted **FING** off my finger? The pain is excruciating."

"Yes, yes, yes, of course, my darling," replied Mother. "Myrtle, would you be a dear and help me pull the **FING** off your father's finger, please?"

"NO!" snapped the girl. "You do it, you lazy old moo!"

The lady sighed before grabbing the **FING** with both hands. The creature's eye swivelled round to give her a dirty look.

"Heave!" ordered Mr Meek.

Mrs Meek did her absolute best heaving, but the **FING** did not budge an inch.

"Heave!"

Again nothing.

"HEAVE!"

Nothing.

The poor lady was pooped.

"I am so sorry, Father, but I am all heaved out!" she sighed.

Father had an idea. "Have you got any **custard creams** in the house?"

"No," replied Mother. "Not one. We did have a whole tin, but the **FING** scoffed them all in seconds."

That gave Father an idea. "Then that must be the only way to get this wretched thing off!" he announced. "With a –" he paused for effect –

"BISCUIT!"

Chapter 24

BEING BRITISH

Mr Meek drew some funny looks in the supermarket, what with the **FING** still biting on to him. **Being British,** he thought it best to carry on as if there were absolutely nothing at all strange about having a furry ball with one eye stuck to the end of his finger.

He greeted his fellow shoppers with a smile. "Good morning!"

Being British, they didn't say anything. Instead they just smiled weakly and hurried off as fast as they could.

Despite being far too big to sit in the baby seat on the shopping trolley, Myrtle insisted on squeezing herself into it.

"I'm allergic to walking!" she announced as

her parents lowered her in.

"Now, where are the **custard creams?**" asked Father.

"I want crisps!" demanded Myrtle.

"No, we are not getting crisps today, my fluffy kitten," replied Mother. "Just **custard creams** so we can get that **FING** off your poor father's finger."

Myrtle never, ever did what her parents said, and she wasn't going to start now. So the girl grabbed a bumper bag of crisps and dropped it into the trolley.

D

   I   N

        K!

"Just those, then, light of my life," said Mother. "Nothing else."

"MORE! MORE! MORE!"

"No more, please!"

"CHOCOLATE!"

"No, we are not getting any chocolate today, bunny wunny," replied Father.

Myrtle grabbed the biggest bar of chocolate from the shelf.

CLUNK!

"That's all now, please, dearest heart," said Father, picking up the pace and pushing the trolley as fast as he could to get to the biscuit section. The **FING** must have been getting hungry. Perhaps it was smelling all the food. Its eye widened and its sharp teeth sank deeper and deeper into Mr Meek's finger.

"GRRR!" it growled.

"MOOBOOFOOBOODOODOO!" cried Mr Meek in pain.

"MORE! MORE! MORE!"

"I said no more, please," pleaded Mother.

"SWEETS!"

"No, we are not getting any sweets today, poppet!" she spluttered as she desperately tried to keep up with the speeding trolley.

Mr Meek was now pushing it so fast that old ladies had to leap out of the way.

"Sorry!" he exclaimed as some poor old dear landed in the deep freeze.

"Please don't apologise!" she called back. "I needed some frozen peas!"

All the time, Myrtle was grabbing bags and bags and bags of sweets and dropping them into the trolley.

DINK! DUNK! DENK!

Soon it was overflowing with goodies.

"No more sweets, boo-boo!" said Mr Meek as he now sprinted down the aisle. He began to feel light-headed with the pain. It felt as if the **FING** was going to bite his poor finger off.

"GRRRRR!"

"BIBBITY-BOBBOTY-BOO!" yelled Father.

Just then a bulky security guard trundled round the corner and barked,

"STOP THAT TROLLEY!"

Chapter 25
WART

Unwisely, the security guard was standing right in the path of the speeding trolley. Even though her hand was in a STOP position, Mr Meek just couldn't bring it to a halt.

"SORRY!" he cried out, but it was too little too late.

BOINK!

The trolley with Myrtle still sitting in it bashed into the security guard, sending her flying.

WHIZZ!

"UGH!"

"HUH! HUH!" laughed the girl.

"It's not funny, darling," corrected Mother.

"No, it's hilarious!" was the reply. "HUH! HUH! HUH!"

The security guard landed in the cheese section between a *Blue Wensleydale* and a **RED LEICESTER**. Fortunately, a soft cheese, a **Stinking Bishop**, cushioned her landing.

SPLAT!

"OOF!"

"Super cheese selection," remarked Mr Meek with a

smile. He was hoping that he could somehow distract the security guard from her mentioning being run over by a man with a furry ball on the end of his finger.

"Would you care to explain where you were going in such an unholy hurry?" demanded the security guard as she wiped the stinky goo from her bottom.

"We were just making a slow amble over to the biscuits!" replied Mr Meek, pointing with his finger, momentarily forgetting that he still had the **FING** attached to it.

"O o p s ,"
he muttered.

"What's that?"
demanded the guard.

"What's what?" was
the mock-innocent
reply.

"That thing."

"It's a **FING**," interjected Myrtle.

"SHUSH!" shushed the girl's mother.

"Pets are strictly forbidden in this supermarket," announced the guard.

"It's not a pet," fibbed Father.

"Would you care to explain what it is, then?"

Mr Meek thought for a moment. He wasn't good at lying. "A **wart**."

"A **WART**! HUH! HUH! HUH!" laughed Myrtle.

"SHUSH!" shushed Mother.

The security guard did not look convinced. She leaned in to inspect the protuberance. As she got closer, her eyes narrowed and her nose wrinkled in disgust. "If it is a **wart**, it is the **biggest, hairiest,** most **repulsive-looking** wart I have ever seen in my life."

"Thank you," replied Mr Meek. "My **wart** has won competitions."

The **FING'S** eye opened, and swivelled to look at the security guard.

"AND IT'S GOT AN EYE!"

"That's probably why it won."

The guard looked most disturbed, and demanded, "What kind of competitions?"

"**Wart** competitions, obviously. It won first prize for furriest wart in the south-west region. I got a certificate. And my **wart** here got a rosette."*

The **FING** must have heard all this talk about being a **wart**, because it snarled and sank its teeth in deeper.

"GRRR!"

"NANANANANANANANANANANANA NANANANANANANA!"

"Your **wart** just growled!" exclaimed the guard.

"Did it? I didn't hear anything," lied Mr Meek.

"It most certainly did."

"GRRR!"

"SUDOKU!"

"There it goes again!"

---

* *Wart competitions were incredibly popular in medieval times, when having a face consisting entirely of warts was considered the height of beauty.*

"Large **warts** do make a noise," lied Mr Meek. "It is best not to be alarmed. It just means they are growing. Now, if you'll excuse me and my **wart**, we really must pick up that packet of *custard creams*. Goodbye!"

With that, he thrust the trolley forward, and was gone.

WHIZz!

Chapter 26

A VOLCANIC EXPLOSION OF TEARS, SNOT AND DRIBBLE

With his free hand, Mr Meek snatched a packet of *custard creams,* and raced to the nearest till. When all the items Myrtle had grabbed had passed along the conveyor belt, the moody teenage cashier announced, **"That's seven hundred and eighty-three pounds and fifty-three pence!"**

That was a colossal haul of crisps, chocolates and sweets. Even for Myrtle.

"But I don't have that much money on me," panicked Mr Meek.

"Nor me," yelped Mrs Meek. She turned to her daughter. "Beauteous one, do you mind awfully if we put back a bag or two of sweeties?"

Myrtle looked at her parents with utter contempt.

"NOOOOOOOOOOOOOOOOOOOOOOOOOOOOOOOOOOOOOOOOOOOOOOOOOOOOOOOOO!"

she screamed.

It was so loud everyone in the supermarket could hear. In fact, it was so loud everyone in the supermarket in the next town could hear too. Of course, being meek by name and meek by nature, the last thing Mr and Mrs Meek wanted was to make a scene. Even **FING** didn't like it. The creature growled…

"GGGGGGGGRRRRRR!!!!!!!"

…closed its one eye and bit hard on Father's finger again.

He winced. "MINTYMUNTYMONTY!" As all eyes turned to the shy little man, he added,

"Apologies, my **wart** is just going through a growth spurt."

"**GRRR!**" **FING** didn't like that. Oh no. The creature bit harder still.

"**YABBADABBADOO!**" yelped Father. "Please, we need to get home, and fast. Let's just put back this industrial-sized tin of fudge?"

He reached into the trolley for it.

"DON'T TOUCH THE FUDGE!"

"What if I do?" asked Father.

"I WILL SCREAM AND SCREAM AND SCREAM UNTIL I THROW UP ALL OVER YOU!"

"She's done it before," mused Mother.

Now a queue of disgruntled shoppers was forming behind the Meek family. Being British, although no one was openly complaining at having to wait, there was an awful lot of tutting.

"**TUT!**"

"**TUT!**"

"**TUT!**" tutted the tutters.

"Oh no. We are being tutted at. This is horrendously embarrassing," whispered Father.*
"Please could we put back just this one incy wincy ickle bag?" begged Mother, holding up a humble packet of toffees.

"WWWWWWWWWWWAAAAAAAA AAHHHHHHHHHHH!" wailed Myrtle.

---

* *Tutting was invented by King Tut, or Tutankhamun, the Ancient Egyptian pharaoh. Every day he would go to see his pyramid being built, and tut loudly if any of his slaves stopped for a tea break.*

A volcanic explosion of tears and snot and dribble sprayed over everyone. Mr and Mrs Meek. **FING.** The cashier. The queue. All were coated from head to toe in Myrtle's tears-snot-dribble gloop.

"GRRR!" growled **FING.**

"Grumble, grumble, grumble," grumbled the crowd of shoppers.

"That was refreshing," remarked Mother, trying to put a positive spin on having been well and truly snotted.*

Because of the commotion, the supermarket manager came charging out of her office.

"OUT! OUT! OUT! GET OUT OF MY SUPERMARKET! AT ONCE!" she shouted. However, the tears-snot-dribble gloop had coated the floor, making it as slippery as an ice rink. This meant her authority was immediately undermined by her slipping over and completing the last part of the journey on her bottom.

WHOOSH!

---

* *Look the word up in* The Walliamsictionary. *It does exist. Snotted means bogeyed, phlegmed or boogered.*

"WOOH!"

She was sliding so fast that she hit the trolley with a...

THUNK!

...sending it thundering forward...

BOOMF!

It crashed straight through the supermarket window...

SMASH!

...sending Myrtle and all the shopping zooming off down the street.

W H O O S H !

"Oh deary, deary me," remarked Mother.

"Oh deary, deary, deary us indeed," added Father.

Chapter 27
CUSTARD-CREAM-INDUCED FRENZY

Myrtle was still squashed into the baby seat, munching on crisps, as the shopping trolley weaved in and out of the path of the oncoming traffic.

BEEP! BEEP!

SCREECH!

HONK! HONK!

SHUNT!

"Stop that trolley!" called Father out of the window of his little car. "It contains some very important *custard creams!*"

"And our daughter!" shouted Mother.

"Oh yes, and our daughter."

"Let's be mindful of the billing. We don't want to upset our little angel."

"Oh yes, Myrtle first."

"Of course!"

Mr Meek swerved the car through the traffic so it was now parallel with the trolley.

BRMM!

"Grab hold of the bonnet!" he ordered Myrtle.

"I'm busy," replied the girl. To be fair, she was busy as she had just popped open the packet of **custard creams.**

"Please don't eat them all, my petal!" pleaded Father, reaching out of the window to grab hold of the trolley. "I need them for **FING!**"

"**GRRR!**" came a growl. **FING'S** eye swivelled and zoomed in on the biscuits.

The sight of them sent the creature into a CUSTARD-CREAM-INDUCED FRENZY.

"GRRRRRRRRRRRRR!"

Immediately, **FING** stopped biting Father's finger.

"GRRR!"

"My finger's still there!" exclaimed Father, inspecting the deep bite marks on his digit.

Then **FING** leaped from the speeding car on to the trolley.

DOINK!

"GRRR!"

It rolled over the packets of food…

RUSTLE! RUSTLE! RUSTLE!

…before leaping at the girl, snatching a biscuit right out of her hand.

CHOMP!

"GET OFF ME, YOU FILTHY LITTLE BEAST!" shouted Myrtle, bashing the creature away with one hand as she helped herself to another *custard cream* from the packet with the other. In all the commotion, she failed to see what was ahead.

A double-decker bus in the middle of the road.

Mr Meek stamped on the brakes of his little car.

SCREECH!

It came to a juddering halt.

Mr and Mrs Meek's faces squashed against the windscreen.

SQUELCH?

"MYRTLE! LOOK OUT!" screamed Mother.

It was too late.

The supermarket trolley walloped into the bus.

BOOSH!

In the blink of an eye, the trolley and all its contents were sailing over the bus and flying through the air.

WHIRR!

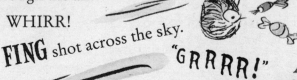

FING shot across the sky. "GRRRR!"

Mr and Mrs Meek looked on, open-mouthed in wonder, as they saw their daughter somersaulting while still eating a biscuit.

MUNCH!

Until the girl landed on the road with an almighty…

KER-THUMP!

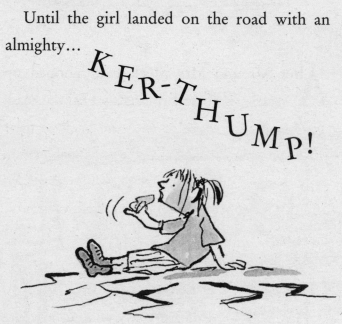

Chapter 28
GOBBLE!

After Mr and Mrs Meek had scooped up Myrtle, **FING** and all the food off the road, and bundled everything into the back of their little car, they drove home. It was only when they opened the boot that they realised **FING** had not just devoured all the *custard creams*.

"Oops!" said Father.

"Oops indeed," agreed Mother.

Oh no.

FING had eaten all the crisps, all the chocolate and all the cake too. It had chocolate all around its mouth. Well, one can only assume it was its mouth. Indeed, we can only assume it was chocolate. Having eaten all the mountain of food from the supermarket, **FING** was now munching its way through the spare tyre.*

GOBBLE!

As a result of all this eating, **FING** had dramatically expanded. It was now around the size of a space hopper. And, just like a space hopper, it bounced.

B O I N K !

It bounced out of the boot.

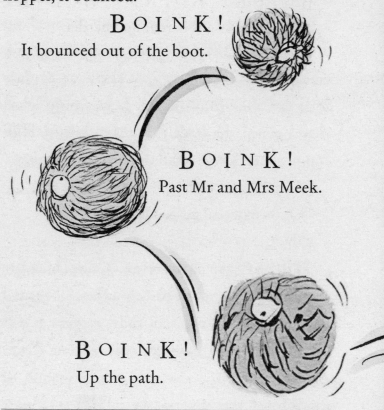

B O I N K !

Past Mr and Mrs Meek.

B O I N K !

Up the path.

---

* *Tyres are not recommended eating. They do tend to taste a tiny bit rubbery.*

B O I N K !

Until it reached the front door.

B O I N K !

As **FING** couldn't go any further now, it bounced and bounced against the door.

B O I N K ! B O I N K ! B O I N K !

The BOINKs got harder and harder.

B O I N K ! B O I N K ! B O I N K !

"Just one moment, please, **FING!**" called out Mother. "I will get that door open in a jiffy!"

It was the best she could do, as sadly she didn't speak **FING.** The lady chased after the creature, jangling the front-door keys. Just as she had the key ready to put in the lock…

B O I N K ! B O I N K ! B O I N K !

…**FING** bounced against the door with such force that it flew off its hinges.

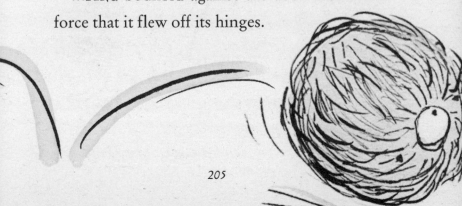

BASH!

The door toppled into the house.

THUD!

"Oh! I see you have the door open already," remarked Mother as cheerfully as she could muster.

Meanwhile, Father lifted Myrtle out of the car. The girl had got even heavier in the weeks since he'd been on his adventure.

"Ooh, my back!" he yelped in pain as he tried to take her weight alone. "Do you mind walking the two or three steps to the house just this once, my petal?"

"NO!" she snapped.

"Well, I'll do my best," sighed Father.

As he staggered past the boot with Myrtle in his arms, she peered in and saw the empty food packages.

"WHERE'S ALL ME GRUB?"
she demanded.

"My dearest one, I have some rather upsetting news..."

"WOT?"

"I am afraid **FING** ate it all."

"NOOOOOOOOO!"

"It didn't *quite* finish the spare tyre, if you fancied a nibble..."

"WwWAAAHHH!"

Now, dear reader, I invite you to regard this splendid heart-warming scene. In the living room, **FING** was bouncing excitedly next to the cage that housed the other **FING** from the pet shop.

BOINK! BOINK! BOINK!

Mother looked on with delight. "How super!" she squealed. "Big **FING** just can't wait to meet Little **FING**!"

Little **FING** had emerged from under a pile of newspaper, and was pressing its mouth (or perhaps its other end*) up against the bars of its cage. Big **FING** banged against it as it bounced.

---

* We will never really know.

"EEK! EEK! EEK!" it squeaked.

BOINK! BOINK! BOINK!

TING! TING! TING!

With some difficulty, Father lugged his daughter into the room, and deposited her on the sofa.

THUMP!

A cloud of dust filled the room.

"These two adorable creatures are going to be the best of friends!" said Mother. "Look, Myrtle dearest!"

"WOT?"

"As they are your pets, perhaps you'd like to introduce Big **FING** to Little **FING**?"

"CARTOONS!"

"Now?"

"YES, NOW!"

Mother sighed, and switched on the television. Myrtle stared at it, picking her nose idly.

"I know from studying all the animal-behaviour books* in the **LIBRARY** that when introducing one pet to another it is sensible to take things very slowly," began Mrs Meek.

"Excellent point, Mother."

"Thank you kindly, Father. You hold on to **Big FING** while I gently take Little **FING** out of its cage."

Mr Meek did what he was told. He kneeled down, slightly snagging his long beard under his knees.

"OUCH!"

"Are you all right?"

"Yes, yes, I am fine!" he replied sharply. Then

---

* *The best book on how to introduce pets to one another is called* How to Introduce Pets to One Another.

he pinned Big **FING** to the carpet to stop it from bouncing.

"GRRRRR!"

Meanwhile, Mrs Meek gently opened Little **FING'S** cage.

TWANG!

"EEK! EEK! EEK!"

"Right," she said as she reached in. "I am just going to let them sniff each other first."

Mother cupped her hand over Little **FING**, who was only the size of a marble. Slowly, slowly, slowly, she brought the creature down to meet the newest member of the family. Little **FING'S** eye widened.

"Little **FING**, meet Big F—" but, before she could say "**ING**", Big **FING** burst out of Father's grip, bounced up...

"GRRRRRRRRRRRRRRRRRRR!"

B O I N K !

...and...

CHOMP!

...devoured Little **FING** in one gulp.

GuRGLe!

"Mmm. That didn't quite go to plan," remarked Mother.

Perhaps the scene wasn't as heart-warming as I had hoped. Apologies.

Chapter 30
INSTANT REPLAY

"Myrtle darling?" began Mother.

"WOT?" replied the girl, still glued to the television.

"It's Little **FING**. There's no nice way to put this... It's been, well..."

"WOT?"

"...eaten."

"NOOOOOOOOOOOOOOOOOOOOOOO!" wailed Myrtle.

"We should have got her a pet-bereavement counsellor," hissed Father.

"My poor, poor angel," said Mother. "You must be very sad."

"YEAH!" exclaimed Myrtle. "Sad I missed it!"

"Excuse me?"

"I WANT AN INSTANT REPLAY!"

"A what?"

"DUH! Get **Big FING** to sick it up, and then gobble it down again."

Tears welled in Mother's eyes, and she put her handkerchief over her mouth. She had never heard anything so stomach-churningly disgusting.

"No!" she said firmly. "We certainly can't do that."

"Then shut your cake hole! Let me finish my **CARTOON."**

"Of course, my angel. I am so sorry for disturbing you!"

"SHUT UP!"

Mrs Meek then turned back to Mr Meek. She noticed something was very wrong.

"Father?"

"Yes, Mother?"

"Where is **FING?**"

The man looked around the living room. The creature was nowhere to be seen.

"Oh no. I don't know!"

BANG!

There it was!

Smashing through the door to the kitchen.

"It must still be hungry," said Father.

The pair raced into the kitchen. They watched in horror as **FING** destroyed everything in sight in its quest for food.

"GRRRRRRRRRRRRRRRRRRRR!"

Plates smashed on the floor. CLATTER!

Pots and pans were sent flying.

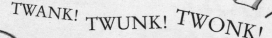

TWANK! TWUNK! TWONK!

Glasses shattered.

CHINKING!

Using one of its ends, **FING** opened the fridge door.

CLICK!

Once inside, it hoovered up everything.

GURGLE! GOBBLE! SCHTOOZLE!

"Make it stop!" screamed Mother. "I was saving that chocolate mousse for Myrtle's tea."

TOO LATE!

SLURP!

It was gone in half a second.

Father went to grab **FING** as it bounced out of the fridge, but it bashed straight into him, knocking him to the ground.

"GGGGGGGGRRRRRRRRRRR!!!!!!!"

BOFF!

"OOF!"

THUD!

"No!" screamed Mother. She jumped on top of **FING,** sitting on it.

"I don't believe it. I am sitting on **FING!**" she exclaimed.

"GRRR!"

The creature looked up menacingly before rolling every which way to try to escape.

"GRRR! GRRR! GRRR!"

Still Mother pushed down with her bottom.

"TAKE THAT!"

All of a sudden, **FING** stopped completely still.

"Oh no! I've **killed** it!"

exclaimed Mother.

PART FIVE

KABOOM!

Chapter 31
PONG

All was silent, until the creature closed its one eye in concentration, and let out a deafening sound.

FURT!

The sound was followed by an almighty dropping being dropped.

THUD!

It was so almighty that it was actually larger than **FING** itself.

Picking himself up from the floor, Father admired the dropping. "How is that even possible?"

"I don't know," replied Mother, "but at least we know now which end is which. Poor Little **FING** must be in there somewhere."

"Well, I am afraid to say that there's not much hope for it now, Mother," said Father, joining his wife as she peered at the dropping.

"No."

"No, indeed."

A smell so wretched that it began peeling the paint off the walls filled the room.*

It was so vile that even **FING'S** eye watered. Poor Mrs Meek covered her mouth with her handkerchief. **"FING'S** thing pongs."

"Don't you fret, Mother! I will dispose of it!" replied Father as he reached into the cupboard for the dustpan and brush. However, as soon as he brought them out, he realised they were laughably small for the task.

"Let me!" said Mother.

With that, she held her breath and pushed the dropping out of the kitchen and into the garden.

TRUNDLE!

TRONDLE!

TRINDLE!

"There!" she said, brushing her hands together at a job well done.

"Well done, Mother."

"Thank you, Father."

---

* *HANDY HINT: Fing droppings actually make an inexpensive alternative to paint remover.*

Then the pair stared at **FING,** who
was now devouring the Meeks' family
selection of breakfast cereals, boxes and all.
MUNCH! **CRUNCH!** FUNCH!
All the time growing bigger

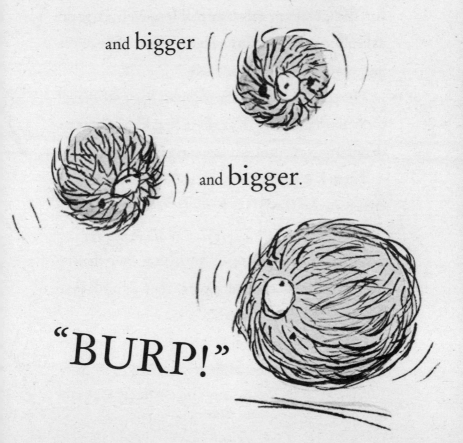

and bigger

and bigger.

"BURP!"

"What on earth are we going to do with it?" asked Father.

Mother thought for a moment. "Could you take it back?"

"Take it back?"

"To where you found it?"

"I nearly died getting it here!"

"Well, I worry what might happen to Myrtle if **FING** stays. If it did one of its droppings on her, she could be buried alive."

The pair looked lost in thought for a moment. Only for a moment, though. They were too nice to entertain the notion any longer.

Then Father had an idea. "How about we lock it in the shed?"

"Myrtle?"

"No. **FING.**"

"Yes. Yes. Of course. I knew that. I think that is a splendid idea, Father."

"Thank you kindly, Mother."

"**GRRR!**" growled **FING**. Its one eye narrowed.

The creature didn't like the idea one bit. So, as fast as it could, it bounced out of the kitchen into the hallway.

B O I N K !

B O I N K !

B O I N K !

"Oh no!"
said Father.
"It's on the move!"

Chapter 32
FIZZLING FUR

As their daughter carried on happily watching **CARTOONS** in the living room, Mr and Mrs Meek chased **FING** all over the house.

It bounced up the stairs…

B O I N K !

B O I N K !

B O I N K !

…knocking the pictures off the walls.

"GRRRRRRRRRRRRRR!"

It bounded into the bedroom and bounced up and down on the bed.

B O I N K !
B O I N K !
B O I N K !

The bed broke in two. CRUNCH!

"GRRRRRRRRRRRRRR!"

"PLEASE, **FING,** NO!" cried Mr and Mrs Meek. Try as they might, they just couldn't stop it.

B O I N K !   B O I N K !   B O I N K !

Next, it bounded into the bathroom and bounced up and down on the loo.

B O I N K !
B O I N K !
B O I N K !

It shattered the bowl.

CRACK! CRUNCH! KERCHINK!

"GRRRRRRRRRRRRRRRRRRR!"

"NO!"

Loo water began splurging everywhere.

SPLATTER!

Mr and Mrs Meek were soaked to the skin.

"URGH!"

BOINK! BOINK! BOINK!

It bounced into Myrtle's room, smashing all her things to pieces.

BISH! BASH! BOSH!

"GRRRRRRRRRRRRRR!"

Remote-controlled hedge. Smashed.

Nelson's Column made out of sultanas. Broken.

Solid-gold hamster wheel. Ruined.

Giant inflatable walnut. Burst.

Wombat juicer. Destroyed.*

"**FING,** STOP!

WE BESEECH YOU!" shouted Mother.

---

* *This was good news for wombats as generally they don't enjoy getting juiced. Well, would you?*

"GRRRRRRRRRRRR RRRRRR!"

Having nothing left to destroy on the top floor, **FING** bounced back down the stairs.

BOINK! BOINK! BOINK!

Going at quite a speed, **FING** bashed into the living-room door...

THUNK!

...smashing it to pieces.

KERUNCH!

"GRRRRRRRRRRRRRR!"

Then it bounced over Myrtle, who was spread out on the sofa...

BOINK! "OI!"

...before coming to a halt as it smashed into the television screen.

CRASH!

FIZZLE!

The television exploded.

KABOOM!

"WAH!" screamed the girl. "NOW I CAN'T WATCH MY *CARTOON!*"

As her parents dashed into the living room, a singed **FING** plopped out of the television.

DUNK!

Electricity fizzled all over its fur.

FIZZLE! FAZZLE! FUZZLE!

"GET THAT **FING** OUT OF HERE!"
ordered Myrtle. To add emphasis to her rage,
the girl stamped her feet.

STOMP!

STOMP!

STOMP!*

With the creature stunned, Mr and Mrs Meek
seized their chance.

---

* *Myrtle only had two feet, not three. She stamped
her right foot once and her left foot twice, hence the
three stomps. Apologies for any confusion. If Myrtle
did have three feet, I am pretty sure I would have
mentioned it earlier.*

"NOW!" ordered Mother.

The pair pounced on it. They rolled **FING** into the garden. With all their might, they squished it through the shed door, and locked it.

CLUNK!

Together they held hands and skipped back into the house. Little did they know what horror was in store for them during the night.

WAH! HA! HA! HA!*

---

* *That is an evil laugh.*

KABOOM!

The noise of the explosion woke up everyone in the street.

Mr and Mrs Meek lurched upright in their beds, as if waking from a nightmare.

"What was that, Mother?" asked Mr Meek.

"I don't know, Father."

"One of us had better go out and look."

"Yes."

There was an uncomfortable silence. Of course, neither of them wanted to go out and look.

"So, it's me again, is it?" asked Father.

"Yes! **My hero!**"

"Oh yes. I almost forgot. I am a hero now."

The man gulped, slipped on his slippers, dressed himself in his dressing gown and tiptoed down the stairs. Then, slowly and silently, he opened the back door.

At Father's feet was a shard of wood that looked strangely familiar. As he stepped across the grass, he noticed more and more shards.

"They look exactly like pieces of the shed."

Soon, Mr Meek was standing exactly where the shed should be. Except there was no shed.

What's more, there was no **FING** either.

DUM!

DUM!

DUM!*

All the bits and pieces Father kept in the shed were gone too. The plant pots, the watering can, the spade, the rake, even the lawnmower. At that moment, it finally dawned on the man what must have happened.

"CRIPES!"

"How is everything, Father?" called Mother from the window.

"Not too good, Mother."

"Why is that?"

---

* *That is a dramatic musical sting. Again, like the evil laugh, it will probably work better if read out loud.*

"I think **FING** devoured all my gardening equipment, and then became so big it burst out of the shed!"

"Oh no."

"Oh yes."

"So where is **FING** now?"

"I don't know."

SLUNK!

Myrtle's window slid open, and she hollered out into the garden, "WILL YOU SHUT YOUR CAKE HOLES? IT'S BEDTIME!"

"Sorry, my love heart," called Father. "I feel rotten having to be the bearer of bad news..."

"WHAT NOW?"

"Well, erm, you see…"

"GET ON WITH IT!"

"**FING** has escaped."

"GOOD RIDDANCE!" shouted the girl. "I hate its guts! It broke all me stuff. I hope **FING** gets knocked down by a truck!"

SCREECH!

There was the sound of tyres skidding.

BOOM!

Then, overhead, Father spotted a truck soaring through the air.

ZOOM!

Before it crash-landed on to the roof of their house.

BOOM!

"I think it might be the other way round," said Father.

Chapter 34
ESCAPED BURP

Using all her might, Mother lugged Myrtle out of the house as it collapsed around them.

CRASH! BANG! WALLOP!

In no time, it was nothing more than a pile of bricks.

"Oops," said Father.

"Oops indeed," agreed Mother.

"WwwAAAHHH!" wailed Myrtle. "My stuff! It's broken all my stuff!"

Amongst the rubble Mr Meek spied a jar.

"All is not lost, Myrtle," he began. "You've still got the

jar containing one of Albert Einstein's burps."

As he spoke, he unscrewed the lid and sniffed inside.*

"NOOOO!" she screamed, snatching the jar off him. "You have let the burp escape!"

"Ooh, sorry," he said, and he tried but failed to scoop the invisible burp back into the jar.

Mrs Meek's foot slipped on something.

"Oops!"

Mr Meek put his hand out to steady her.

Looking down, he spotted **THE MONSTERPEDIA**, trying to wriggle free.

---

* *Celebrated physicist Albert Einstein's burps smelled mainly of fried onions.*

"**ACHOO!**" The book sneezed at all the dust.

"Thank goodness **THE MONSTERPEDIA** is not lost! I can take that back to the **LIBRARY** first thing tomorrow. Those fines are mounting! They are already up to **15p**."

As he picked up the book, he noticed something was looming over them.

"**LOOK!**" cried Mother.

FING was now the size of a small moon.

"**GRRR!**" it growled.

Then, like a deadly basketball, it bounced away along the road.

B O I N K ! B O I N K ! B O I N K !

"GRRRRRRRRRRRRRR!"

It destroyed everything in its path.

Cars were crushed.

CRUNCH!

Lampposts were bent.

TWONG!

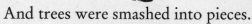

And trees were smashed into pieces.

WHAMP! WHOMP! WHUMP!

All the Meeks' neighbours were waking up and opening their windows to see a huge furry ball bouncing along outside.

"HELP!" one cried.

"CALL THE POLICE!" shouted another.

"STOP THAT HUGE FURRY BALL!" hollered the newsagent Raj, who lived on their street. "AND BRING IT TO MY SHOP! I HAVE SOME SPECIAL OFFERS!"*

---

* *Raj always gets annoyed when I don't include him in a book, so here he is. Happy now?*

The blond-haired boy who lived down the road, Tom, ran out into the street to get a better look at this strange creature.

"Cool!" he said.

What wasn't so cool was that **FING** was about to bounce down on top of him.

WHOOSH!

"GRRRRRRRRRRRRR!"

His golden retriever, Eden, ran into the road, and dragged the boy out of the way just in time.

WALLOP!

The Meek family clambered over the rubble that was their house, staring open-mouthed at the chaos and destruction.

BOOM! SMASH!

SHATTER!

"I think it best we don't mention that **FING** is ours," said Mr Meek.

"We have to do the right thing," urged Mother. "For Myrtle. She really looks up to us."

"No, I don't," snapped the girl.

"Well," said Mother, "we can't just let **FING** destroy the whole town, the whole country, the whole world! We have to go after it!"

"Oh no," replied Mr Meek, before turning to what was left of the car. The windows were cracked, the bonnet crumpled and one of the doors was hanging off.

"I'm going back to bed!" announced Myrtle.

"You don't have one any more," replied Mother.

"OH... YES..."

Mr and Mrs Meek deposited their daughter on to the back seat of the car, and raced off into the night.

Chapter 35
BEHIND YOU

Father flicked on the windscreen wipers to wipe away some bricks, and the car sped off down the road in pursuit of **FING**.

BRUM!

RATTLE!

Debris hit the car as they followed in the creature's wake.

A bicycle smashed through the windscreen.

"Ah! Fresh air!" remarked Mother, once again trying to put a positive spin on things.

"FASTER! FASTER! FASTER!" screamed Myrtle from the back seat. **"MORE! MORE! MORE!"**

"I am going nearly twenty miles per hour!" protested Father.

"I SAID FASTER!" she yelled. To add emphasis, she whacked him on the side of his head with her slipper.

THWACK!

"OW!"

"MORE! MORE! MORE!"

His foot stamped down on the accelerator, and the car dramatically sped up to twenty-five miles per hour.

VVVRRROOOMMM!

It actually overtook **FING.**

"Goodness me, where is it?" said Mother, poking her head out of the window.

Father checked the rearview mirror. "It's behind us!"

DOOF!

FING bounced down on the roof with such force that the little car fell to pieces completely.

CLANK! CLUNK! CLINK!

Soon the three Meeks were skidding along the road on their car seats.

WHIZZ!

Father was still holding on to the steering wheel, though now it wasn't attached to anything.

"Mother, I think the car may need to go into the garage," he remarked as one of the back wheels rolled past him.

TRUNDLE!

As if all this wasn't humiliating enough for Father, Myrtle struck him on the other side of his head with her slipper.

THWACK!

"STOP THE CAR!"

she ordered.

Mr Meek put his foot down to press the brake. It wasn't there any more. Instead his foot hit the road.

"ARGH!"

Because of the friction, his slipper burned off and his poor foot began to glow like molten lava. At least it did slow him down, causing Myrtle to crash straight into the back of him.

WALLOP!

"OOF!"

They then smashed into the back of Mother.

BASH!

"OUCH!"

Soon the Meek family was lying in a crumpled heap on the road.

"That wasn't too bad," said Mother.

Myrtle, who was at the bottom of the pile, begged to differ.

"You are squashing me, you great fat oafs!"

Her parents rolled off her, and she looked up to the sky.

"Oh no!" she muttered, seeing FING'S eye

bulging with glee,

a second away from

crashing

down

upon

her.

Chapter 36

A GINORMOUS BOOT UP THE BOTTOM

Mr and Mrs Meek grabbed an arm each in a desperate attempt to pull their daughter to safety. Because they pulled in opposite

directions, Myrtle went nowhere. Just as the creature was about to make impact and turn the girl into jelly, Myrtle kicked up her leg and booted **FING** as hard as she could.

"TAKE THAT, YOU BEAST!"

"GRRRR!" it cried.

It was impossible to know which end her foot had struck. It might have been a boot in the mouth, or it might have been a boot in the bottom.*

Either way, it worked. **FING** flew up into the air…

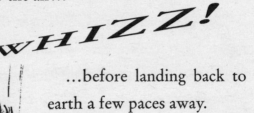

WHIZZ!

…before landing back to earth a few paces away.

PLOP!

Rather sorrowfully, it rolled to a stop at the end of the road and let out a pitiful yelp.

"YAP! YAP! YAP!"

A large tear, around the size of a football, welled up in its eye and trickled down its fur.

---

* *I wouldn't recommend either.*

"HA! HA!" mocked Myrtle. "It's nothing but a great big scaredy-cat!"*

Feeling all full of herself now, the girl waddled over to the creature.

WADDLE! WIDDLE! WUDDLE!

"I wouldn't go near it if I were you, darling one," cautioned Father.

"Come back, please, bunnykins," pleaded Mother.

"SHUT YOUR FACES!" was the charming reply. "I'm gonna give it another ginormous boot up the bottom! And this time it's really gonna hurt!"

"GRRRRRRRRRRRR!" growled FING, and its eye narrowed.

This time, it was ready. When the girl kicked up her leg, its mouth widened. (Let's please assume it was not its bottom this time.)

CHOMP!

It locked on to her ankle.

---

* *I know any cats reading this will accuse me of being cattist for using this phrase. Apologies.*

"ARGH!" said the girl. "IT'S GOT ME FOOT!"

Mr and Mrs Meek rushed over to extract their daughter from **FING'S** grasp.

"**FING,** STOP!" shouted Father.

"PLEASE, **FING!** I IMPLORE YOU!" joined in Mother.

However, before they could reach her, **FING** began rolling down the road at terrific speed, taking Myrtle with it.

Every time **FING**
completed a circle,
Myrtle was rolled over.

"WAH!
WAH!

WAH!" she wailed
as the weight of the
ginormous **FING**
squashed her.

Father and Mother chased after them, but the
creature rolled faster and faster.

WHIZZ!

The "WAH!" "WAH!" "WAH!"s came
faster and faster too.

Soon **FING** was rolling so speedily that the
pair became a blur. *BLLLLUUUUUUURRRRR!*

"I've got a stitch!" complained Father.

Mother stopped to comfort him. "Poor you!"

After just a few seconds, **FING** and Myrtle were far away. In a few seconds more, they had completely disappeared.

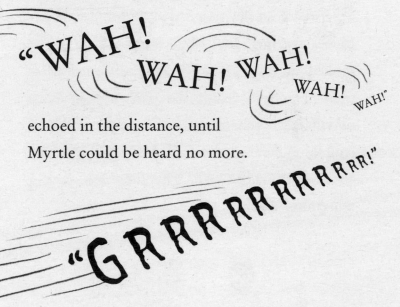

"WAH! WAH! WAH! WAH! WAH!"

echoed in the distance, until Myrtle could be heard no more.

"GRRRRRRRRRR!"

"Goodbye, sweetest of sweet cheeks!" called out Mother.

"Farewell, my angel sent from heaven!" called out Father.

There followed a sound Mr and Mrs Meek hadn't heard for a long, long time. Not since the day Myrtle had been born.

The sound of silence.

The pair smiled. For the first time in years, a sense of peace descended upon them. Mr Meek reached for Mrs Meek's hand. She looked at him lovingly, and he squeezed it tight. Hand in hand, the pair walked back to whatever was left of their house. And, of course, to finally take **THE MONSTERPEDIA** back to the **LIBRARY**. The fine was now a whopping **20p**.

Chapter 37
SILENCE

Months passed with absolutely no sign of Myrtle. There were no sightings of her anywhere, despite Mr and Mrs Meek putting up a poster in the window of the **LIBRARY**.

Of course, they wanted their daughter back safely. Life just wasn't the same without her, even though now they

OUR DARLING DAUGHTER IS MISSING.

HAVE YOU SEEN MYRTLE?
NO NEED TO TELEPHONE.
A LETTER WILL SUFFICE.
A SECOND-CLASS STAMP IS FINE.
NO RUSH.
THANK YOU KINDLY.

didn't have to carry the great lump to school. Now they didn't have to buy a tonne of chocolate every week. Now they could read their beloved poetry books in peace. Now they could wake up in the morning to the birds singing in the trees rather than the sound of Myrtle howling. Now they could watch things other than **CARTOONS** on the television.

EPILOGUE

In fact, it wasn't until they were watching a nature programme one evening some years later that Mr and Mrs Meek finally discovered what had happened to their daughter.

"Here, in the deepest, darkest, jungliest jungle," began the safari-suited expert in hushed tones, "we can see all kinds of curious creatures that we thought had died out many years ago."

"That is where I found **FING!**" exclaimed Father, nearly spitting out his tea. He and his wife were sitting in their caravan, which was parked exactly where their house used to stand. Sadly, the house was still a pile of rubble.

"There might be a clue to the whereabouts of our beauteous daughter," replied Mother.

The pair leaned forward on the sofa.

On the screen, the expert continued his commentary. "This patch of the Earth, so remote that even we don't know where we actually are, is home to all sorts of creatures that our forefathers thought were monsters, and which have only been written about in a long-lost ancient book entitled **THE MONSTERPEDIA.**"

"That's the book from the vaults of the **LIBRARY!**" said Father, dunking a *custard-cream* biscuit into his tea.

"Behold these creatures, which have never, ever been captured on camera before.
Look, there is a **honkopotamus**.

That is a flock of **wong-wing birds**.

The two-headed reptilian creature is a **croco-croco**.

And, just buzzing over my head, which is why the Earth is now entirely in shadow, is the flying **helephant**. However weird and wonderful you think these creatures are, nothing compares to the **FING**."

"There it is!" shouted Mr Meek at the television.

Onscreen, the giant furry ball rolled into view. **FING** had grown even bigger, and was now the size of a planet.*

"This colossal and entirely round being has just one eye and an opening at each end, though no one knows which end is which, not even the **FING** itself. Surely this is the most curious creature in the deepest, darkest jungle?"

"YES!" shouted Mr and Mrs Meek back at the television.

The presenter continued. "Well, an animal not even listed in **THE MONSTERPEDIA** is *this* bizarre-looking beast. A creature that, as far as we know, has never, ever been seen by humans before..."

---

* *A small planet. But, still, a planet.*

Mr and Mrs Meek slid off the sofa so their faces were now right next to the television. On the screen appeared an extremely curious

creature indeed. It was impossibly tall and thin, as if it had been flattened, or rolled into shape.

"It is almost human in form," began the expert. "But this is no human being. Caked in mud, it lives in the swamps of the **deepest, darkest, jungliest jungle**, where it feeds on giant worms or pludges. The only sound it makes is **'MORE'!"**

Right on cue, it let out a **"MORE!"**

Mr and Mrs Meek knew that sound.

"MYRTLE!" they screamed.

"Should we try to bring her back?" asked Father.

Mother studied the screen, and watched as Myrtle took a massive chomp out of a giant worm.

CHOMP!

"I think she looks happy enough," replied Mother.

"You are right," he agreed. "Why spoil her fun?"

The onscreen commentary continued. "From what we have observed over the months we have spent here, this creature is by far the most feared in the **deepest, darkest, jungliest jungle.** When it approaches, all the other animals scatter."

True to his word, as Myrtle stomped through the trees…

STOMP!

STOMP!

STOMP!

…the **honkopotamus** used its wind power to shoot off.

PFFFT!

The **helephant** flew into a tree.

B O O M !

And **FING** rolled off in the opposite direction.

However, it wasn't fast enough for Myrtle's long arms. She grabbed hold of the colossal beast.

"**GRRR!**" it growled.

She lifted it above her head…

"**GRRR!**"

…and hurled it right at the presenter.

W H I Z Z

"**GRRRRRRRRRRRRRR!**"

BOOsH!

"ARGH!" the presenter screamed.

Then the screen fizzled to black.

"Oh dear," remarked Mother.

"Oh dear indeed," remarked Father.

The next morning, Mr and Mrs Meek woke up with the feeling that they needed to do something. They weren't sure exactly what. But something. When they arrived at the **LIBRARY** before opening time, the first thing they did was descend the steps to the dark and dingy vaults. There was the dusty old leather-bound book that had started them on this journey, **THE MONSTERPEDIA**.

"Have you got a pen, Father?" asked Mother.

"Here you go, Mother," replied Father, handing her his fountain pen.

The book bounced up on to a table, and opened itself.

FLICK!

The lady found an empty page, and began writing.

Now

THE MONSTERPEDIA

could finally be

complete.

THE LESSER SPOTTED MYRTLE:

A surprisingly flat creature, found only in the **deepest, darkest, jungliest jungle**. It is a swamp dweller, and spends its days eating giant worms, going "MORE!" and generally scaring the life out of all the other animals. The lesser spotted Myrtle is a highly dangerous creature and should NEVER be approached. It is an absolute <u>monster</u>, which is why it belongs only in the pages of this book.

"Excellent work, Mother."

"Thank you, Father."

"A cup of tea and a biscuit?"

"Custard cream?"

"Ooh yes. I don't mind if I do."

So you see, Mr and Mrs Meek really did have a monster for a child. Of course, monsters belong in only one place, the **deepest, darkest, jungliest jungle.** So, children, do make sure you

BEHAVE, or

you might just end up there.

THE END

Here is your very own custard
cream to cut out and keep!